Gray Tide II: Tidal Effects

Andrew J Heller

CONTENTS

INDEX OF ILLUSTRATIONS

Introduction

In *Gray Tide in the East*, I attempted to write a "scientific" alternate history, which is to say, one that was grounded as much as possible in the actual history of the period. It was as much a thought experiment in history as it was a novel, wherein I tried to explore the consequences of one changed historical event in a rigorous way. I wanted to avoid as much as I could wild and wooly speculations, and stay with what could be reasonably supported by historical research.

Gray Tide is, as many readers have said, a short book. The main reason for its brevity is that I was constrained by the self-imposed rules set forth above. It is an elementary proposition of alternate history that the further one travels in time past the changed event (the "point of departure" or "POD," to use alternate history jargon), the more one is forced to speculate, and the less one can rely on actual history. (This is known as the "Butterfly Effect" in AH circles.) The POD for *Gray Tide* occurs in 1914, and the book ends in 1916, because of my to go beyond what I believed the historical sources could support. I also thought the book was fairly complete and reasonably self-contained.

After *Gray Tide* was published, however, numerous reviewers assumed that it was only the first in a planned series, and that there was a sequel in the works. I had no plans for a sequel, as any such project could not be written with the rigor of the original, due to the afore-mentioned Butterfly Effect.

In the end, I capitulated to the demands of my readers, and you are now reading the result. I have tried to apply the methods of the first book to the present one by using actual historical persons in the stories, and by doing my best to base the events herein on the historical record wherever and whenever possible.

FOREWORD

This book is a sequel to my alternate history of the First World War, Gray Tide in the East. *It is not necessary to read the earlier novel to enjoy the stories in this book, although this book does require a brief introduction.*

In Gray Tide in the East, *the history of the Great War changes on August 1, 1914 when the Emperor of Germany, Kaiser Wilhelm II, calls off the long-planned German invasion of Belgium, and orders the right wing of the German Army, 750,000 men, to go East against the Russian Empire, instead of West against France. (The Kaiser actually did cancel the invasion at the last minute, but the Chief of his General Staff, Helmuth von Moltke, persuaded him to reverse his decision).*

The Kaiser's order has a profound effect on the course of the war. The first consequence is that Great Britain does not enter the war. In 1914, Britain had no treaty obligations to any nation in Europe… except Belgium. Under the 1839 Treaty of London, Britain, along with Germany (originally Prussia), France, Russia and Austria had all pledged to defend the perpetual neutrality of Belgium, and to declare war against any power violating that neutrality. It was because of the German violation of Belgian neutrality, and for that reason alone, that the British Empire entered the war.

Great Britain had a very small army at the outset of the war, although it was later to swell into a mass army of millions. However, Britain did have the world's biggest and best navy in 1914, and as soon as war was declared, the Royal Navy instituted a blockade of Germany.

This blockade would by 1918 result in the near-strangulation of the German economy, but it had another, more immediate effect as well.

In response to the British blockade by surface ships, which the German Navy could not duplicate or break, Germany attempted to starve Great Britain by the use of a relatively new weapon, the submarine. The German government declared the waters surrounding the British Isles to be a war zone, and warned that any vessel, whether Allied or neutral entering it would be sunk on sight by German submarines. As a result of this unrestricted submarine warfare, hundreds of Americans were drowned in ships that were torpedoed in the war zone, and dozens of American ships were sent to the bottom of the Atlantic. Eventually, unrestricted submarine warfare was the main reason for the entry of the United States into the war against Germany in 1917.

In Gray Tide in the East, *the Germans do not have to contend with the British blockade, the British Army, or the Americans, because of the cancellation of the invasion of Belgium at the outset. With the weight of its army in the East, Germany quickly smashes the Russian Army and forces Russia out of the war in 1915. In the peace treaty that follows, Germany detaches the Baltic States, Eastern Poland, the Ukraine, Belorussia and Finland from the Russian Empire, and subsequently absorbs all of them except Finland into a greatly expanded German Empire. Germany's main ally, Austria -Hungary, receives portions of the Ukraine and Poland as its share of the spoils.*

France launches several futile attacks on Germany, which achieve nothing and incur heavy casualties. When Germany offers France a soft peace after the defeat of her ally Russia, she has no choice but to accept. Under the terms of the Treaty of Bryn Mawr, mediated by American President Woodrow Wilson, Germany allows France to escape from the war without any indemnities or loss of territory except the transfer of three French colonies to Germany: New Caledonia in the South Pacific, Morocco in North Africa and Martinique in the

Caribbean. It is this last German acquisition, which comes perilously close to violating the Monroe Doctrine, that gives rise to the first story in this book set in 1923, eight years after the end of the Great European War.

Book One
High Tide in Martinique

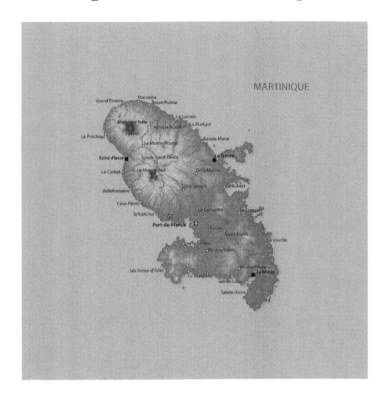

CHAPTER ONE
WASHINGTON, D.C., APRIL 12, 1923

Rear Admiral William Sims read the memorandum again as he waited for the officer he had summoned to arrive at his office. This, the ninth or possibly tenth review of the note was quite unnecessary, as Sims had memorized its contents, but he found that each re-reading stimulated further speculations about the future, a future which he strongly suspected would bring, in the words of the old Chinese curse, "interesting times".

The Chief of Naval Intelligence stroked the neatly trimmed white fringe of beard that decorated his narrow chin as he considered the implications of the State Department memorandum. Leaving aside the whole issue of the Monroe Doctrine, he considered it extremely likely that the British would go berserk if they suspected that Imperial Germany was...

His train of thought was interrupted by a buzz from his intercom. "Lieutenant Commander Spruance is here, but I don't see his name in the appointment book. Shall I send him away?" the tinny-sounding voice of his secretary asked as it emerged from the speaker.

Not for the first time, Sims considered firing his old harridan of a secretary-receptionist. If it were not for the fact that Hilda Davies was the fastest typist and most efficient shorthand scribe in the Navy Department, he would have sacked her long before. He thought about reminding Hilda that she had personally placed Sims' call ordering Spruance to report to his office immediately, and asking her if that did not imply he wanted to see the man right away, and then he shook his head. Trying to get such a woman to understand that there were times to vary from routine was as pointless as trying to teach a mule to dance the Tennessee Waltz. Both were simply unsuited to the task by Nature.

Sims was not aware of the low growling noise he was making as he pushed the intercom button and barked, "No, Miss Davies, send him in to me."

A moment later the door to the inner office opened, and Lieutenant Commander Raymond Spruance entered, his hat tucked under his left arm. He was of unexceptional appearance, with a medium build and height, dark brown hair and brown eyes. But there was something about him, a certain air that suggested there were hidden qualities, not the least of which was a profound intelligence. Sims believed him to be one of the most promising officers in the entire Navy.

"Have a seat, Ray," Sims said, returning the other man's salute and motioning him to a chair. "How is the work coming in your section?" Spruance was assigned to analyzing new weapons being developed by potential rival navies.

After giving the Admiral's question due consideration, Spruance answered, "We're not getting either the quality or quantity of information we need, sir. For example, I would like to have more hard numbers on the range of the new Japanese torpedo, instead of rumors. Also, we still don't know if that new hull the Germans are laying down is intended to be a battle-cruiser or an aircraft carrier, and…"

Sims nodded. "You're going to have to turn those problems over to somebody else for a while. I have a new assignment for you, if you're interested."

Spruance sat up a little straighter at the words "new

assignment." Ever since he had begun his tour of duty at Intelligence, he had made no secret of his desire to return to a shipboard assignment. His stint as C.O. of two destroyers, first *Dale* and later *Osborne*, had been high points of his career, and he would have gladly exchanged his desk in Washington to command a fighting ship again. He would have cheerfully settled for a billet as the executive officer on a cruiser, or possibly on the new aircraft carrier *Langley*.

"If you're looking for a new ship, Ray, I'm afraid I'll have to disappoint you," Sims said. "We need you for intelligence work. You told me you aren't satisfied with the information coming in from our agents; well, neither am I. Today, I was handed this memorandum under the endorsement of the Secretary of the Navy, but which came over from State." He tapped the sheet that lay before him on his desk. "The State Department wants to borrow a naval officer for an investigation."

Spruance raised an eyebrow. The request was unusual, to say the least. The State Department surely had its own sources of information, and he had never heard of them asking for help from Naval Intelligence before.

"It's a small matter, really," Sims continued. "Secretary of State Wood wants somebody to take a trip down to Martinique to have a look around. That somebody should be intelligent, discreet, and a Navy man. Depending on what we find out, it may just mean war with the German Empire. So, are you interested?"

"War?" repeated the startled Spruance. "Is the situation really that serious, sir?"

Sims' expression was stern. "You tell me," he said. He produced a cardboard tube from which he slid a map, which he unrolled on his desk, placing a paperweight on one end and a stapler on the other to keep it flat.

"Our consul down in Wilhelmshaven... that's the capital of Martinique – used to be called Fort-de-France before the Germans took over the island – heard some rumors about a big new port facility being built at a little town called La Trinitie across the island from the capital." Sims jabbed the map with a finger to indicate the locations of the various places named. "Now, the main harbor at Wilhelmshaven handles all the blue-water traffic for the island with ease. In fact, it has a lot more capacity than Martinique needs, because the French built it up a few years before the war with the idea of making it the major trans-shipment port for their Caribbean trade. So what reason would anybody have to develop another deep water port on Martinique, when the one already there can already handle twice the volume of shipping it actually receives?"

Spruance considered the question, his eyes narrowing slightly. "Well, it doesn't sound like a commercial proposition, anyway," he said.

"That's what our man thought, too," Sims agreed. "He made a few inquiries, and confirmed that there is a big construction project underway at La Trinitie. When he asked the German commercial attaché about it, he was told it was a project of the Hamburg-America Line, who wanted to have a modern base for some new Caribbean routes they plan to develop. Oddly enough, neither the commercial attaché nor the Hamburg-America could provide any details. The consul... his name is Welles, by the way... wasn't satisfied with this explanation, so he went over to La Trinitie to see what was going on for himself. The new facility is being built directly across the bay from the old town on the Caravelle Peninsula. They had put up fences all around the land side, and more barriers floating on rafts to obstruct the sea level view."

"It almost sounds as if Hamburg-America has a guilty conscience, or something," Spruance commented.

"Or something," Sims agreed grimly. "The gate to the site was protected by a detachment of armed guards. Welles went over there, identified himself as the American consul and asked to look around in his official capacity."

"Let me guess: they declined to give him the nickel tour," Spruance said.

"Within ten minutes a flunky appeared at the gate to tell Welles that it was completely out of the question because the company was not allowing any unauthorized persons inside until the facility was ready to open. Welles was advised not to return to La Trinitie and was told that if he was found prying around the site again, the colonial Governor would ask the State Department for his recall," Sims said. "Now, what do you think of that?"

"It sounds like a very strange, even eccentric way for a commercial shipping line to treat an official representative of the United States government," Spruance replied slowly. "Of course, if the new port facility is not really a Hamburg-America venture at all, but is in actuality a government project..."

"The German government, let's just say..." Sims interjected.

Spruance nodded his head and continued, "...and that government wanted to keep the facility a secret until it was completed before officially announcing it, so as to present a *fait accompli* to..."

"To the United States, for example..." Sims added.

"...then, I suppose there is a certain logic in trying to keep the new facility under wraps," Spruance finished. "But what could they be building behind those fences that they would need to keep secret, except..." He trailed off.

"Yeah," Sims said. "What could it be other than a brand new base in the Western Hemisphere for the High Seas Fleet?" Sims asked. "And if that is what they're doing down in Martinique, we could be at war with Germany before the leaves fall."

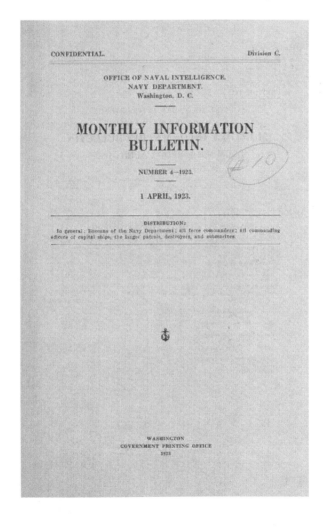

CHAPTER TWO
WILHELMSHAVEN, MARTINIQUE, APRIL 19, 1923

It was hot in Wilhelmshaven, a sweltering 85 degrees under bright sunshine. By the time Ray Spruance reached the end of the long concrete wharf where he had come ashore from the tramp steamer that had brought him to Martinique, sweat had soaked through his shirt to spread in dark patches under the arms of his white linen suit, and had stained the brow of his new Panama hat. He had been expecting it to be hot, but he was unprepared for the suffocating reality of the blazing Caribbean sun combined with sauna-like humidity.

Customs was an open-air wooden shed roofed with palm fronds at the end of the wharf. The casual look of the building suggested an equally casual, perhaps even friendly customs inspection, but Spruance was not surprised to find the German customs officials were neither casual nor friendly. There were only two inspectors to examine the passports and baggage of the more than 30 passengers from the newly arrived ship, and they did not believe in taking half-measures. Each passport was subjected to intense scrutiny and if the contents of each piece of luggage was not put through a painstaking item-by-item examination, it was at least opened and pawed through. As he stood in the line, slowly melting in the tropical heat, Spruance wondered what the customs men thought could possibly be worth smuggling into Martinique. Finally, after a frog-faced official had inspected every page of his passport, including subjecting visas that could not possibly concern him to extended examinations, then groped the contents of Spruance's small leather satchel, he grumpily affixed a stamp, approving his entry into the newest gem in the diadem of freedom in the Caribbean Sea, German Martinique.

Spruance waved off the swarming locals who came down to the docks whenever a ship put in, declining their offers of cabs, hotels and girls. The American consulate was less than a mile from the harbor (indeed, nothing in the little town was much more than a mile from docks), so Spruance decided to walk. It would give him a chance to look the town over and begin to get acclimatized to the island.

The cobblestone streets of the old colonial settlement were narrow and twisting. For the most part there were no sidewalks, so Spruance and other pedestrians had to share the streets with a variety of vehicles ranging from taxis to tiny delivery vans, to bicycles, to donkey carts. He witnessed a number of hair-raising near-collisions as he made his way inland and up the steep hill behind the harbor, but witnessed no actual accidents, or even any serious traffic-related arguments. It appeared that the locals accepted the insane traffic conditions as a matter of course, and were confident that any oncoming car or van would stop or swerve aside rather than run them over.

A few minutes of observation as he walked along persuaded the American that this confidence was justified, so Spruance decided to adopt the local methods. He plowed straight ahead at a steady pace, neither altering his stride or changing direction, even when a Peugeot cycle-car screeched across his path and very nearly ran over his feet. The driver, a young woman wearing a red printed scarf bound around her head from which a few long, blonde hairs had escaped, waved, laughed, and cheerfully fluted, *"Pardonnez-moi, Monsieur!"*

Spruance waved back and replied, *"Ce n'est rien,"* and continued stolidly on his way. After a twenty-five minute walk from the harbor, which included two stops to ask directions, he arrived at his destination: 49 Rue de Saint Pierre.

The consulate was located in a prosperous residential district of large houses, and was much like its neighbors. The consulate building was an airy, white, two-story clapboard converted private house, with covered verandahs wrapping around both floors, big windows and lavish, colorful tropical plantings in front and filling the narrow space with the neighboring buildings. A short, palm-bordered flagstone path led from the street to the base of the steps that went up the front porch.

Spruance walked up to the front door and raised his hand to knock. He hesitated when he saw that the front door was open, and there was only a screen door before him, with nothing solid on which to knock. He looked around for a doorbell, but before he could find it a female voice from inside called, "Come right in, please."

He removed his hat and went in, letting the screen door bang shut behind. He found himself in a large room with a high ceiling. It took a few seconds for his eyes to adjust to the relative dimness of the interior after the bright sunlight on the street. There was a cool breeze blowing in the room, generated by a big fan that circled overhead. In the center of the room was a large oak desk, and seated behind it in a cane-back office chair was the young woman who had invited him inside.

"Please take a seat, sir, and I will assist you in just a moment," the woman said, not looking up from the papers she was examining. She spoke perfect English with a slight trace of a French accent. Spruance remembered her immediately, and when she raised her head and looked at him, her eyes flew wide open in recognition. This was the same woman who had nearly flattened Spruance under the wheels of her little Peugeot a few minutes earlier as he was walking up from the harbor.

"Did you follow me up here make a complaint?" she asked nervously. "Did I injure you, sir? I'm so sorry…"

He laughed and shook his head. "No, no, all you did was create a few seconds of excitement in an otherwise dull existence. My name is Raymond Spruance, and I'm here to see your boss, Consul Welles. Will you please tell him that I'm here?"

The blonde woman sighed with relief when she saw that he that he had not come to report her for her driving. "We were wondering when you would arrive. Mr. Welles is in his private office," she said. "Let me take you back to him."

There was another door, a few feet behind the reception desk. She knocked, and then went in without waiting for permission to enter. "Mr. Welles, Commander Spruance is here."

"Show him in, Elaine," the consul said. As Spruance entered the office, Welles said, "Since his mission is confidential, I think we should refer to our guest as simply 'Mr. Spruance' for the remainder of his stay, Elaine."

"Of course, sir," she agreed. "If you will excuse me, gentlemen," she said, closing the door softly behind her.

The consul rose from behind his desk to offer his hand. "Sumner Welles," he said. "Sorry I wasn't down to meet you at the harbor, but they didn't tell me exactly when you were supposed to arrive. Security, I imagine."

"Ray Spruance," he said, returning the handshake. "Nice to meet you, Mr. Welles." Spruance was pleased with his first impression of the consul. A minor post like this was a dead end that would normally be filled by an older man who had no hope of advancement in the diplomatic service. He would have therefore expected to find a mediocre civil service functionary who was incompetent to handle anything beyond the kind of routine matters that would arise in such an assignment, such as a lost passport or a distressed American traveler. After having read Welles' excellent report to Washington on the German project, however, Spruance had hoped for something more.

Sumner Welles had an air of both intelligence and competence. He appeared to be about Spruance's age, in his late twenties or early thirties. He was dressed neatly in an expensively tailored blue pinstriped seersucker suit. His office, although tiny, with just enough room for a small desk, a pair of chairs for visitors, and a bookshelf, was neat as a pin. The only paper on his desk was a map of the island across which was laid a large magnifying glass. Evidently he had been examining the map when Spruance arrived.

"Have a seat, Mr. Spruance," Welles said. "Since we'll be working together, I might as well tell you a little about myself. If you're wondering why I'm assigned to this backwater, I can assure you that it is not because I'm being punished by State, or that they think I'm an idiot." He paused, as if to give his visitor a chance to deny that he had thought any such thing.

If so, he was disappointed. Spruance said nothing, merely raising an eyebrow in an unspoken question.

"Actually, I normally work at a somewhat higher level. My previous position in the State Department was Assistant Head of the Latin American Division," Welles went on. "I volunteered to come down here as Consul. You see, I have long suspected that Germany was eventually going to attempt to project its power into the Western Hemisphere, and when they did, this colony would be the obvious place to start. So, I thought the Service would need a representative here who was a little more sophisticated in international relations, shall we say, than the usual run of men generally assigned to remote consular posts like this."

Spruance nodded. He was impressed. Welles was a man who had put duty to his country ahead of his personal interests, as he had demonstrated by placing his diplomatic career on hold to volunteer for the lowly position of consul to Martinique.

"By the way, after I found out who they were sending down here, I had my connections in Washington look up your record," Welles went on. "Your efficiency reports are a string of 'outstanding, recommended for promotion.' I asked them for their best man, and I am pleased to see that they sent him."

Spruance was uncomfortable with praise, and was never quite certain how to respond to it. He nodded to acknowledge the compliment, and then asked, "So, do you have any thoughts on how we can get a good look at this new port?"

"I have an idea," Welles answered. "I trust you won't mind a little hike in the hills."

The next morning, they were barreling down a narrow mountain road in bright yellow Citroen coupe, leaving a long plume of dust to mark their passage. The car's maximum speed was 40 miles per hour, but it seemed to Spruance that the consul was taking some of the sharper curves at double that speed. With an effort, he kept his voice casual as he asked, "Are you going to try to get us in through the gate?"

Welles shook his head. "We wouldn't be able to get

anywhere near the front gate. The colonial administration has closed the coast road from La Trinitie to the project site. Without written authorization from the Governor, we couldn't get within a mile of the place. We'll go around the back. Take a look at the map."

Spruance opened the glove box and removed a topographical map of Martinique, which he eventually managed to unfold in the cramped car. It was an excellent map, which had been prepared for the French Army as part of a military survey of the French colonies in 1902. It depicted every road, paved, graveled, or dirt, on the island, including mountain trails used primarily by goats. It also showed changes of elevation in ten meter increments with contour lines.

"We'll stay on the main road and pass south of the town, then pull off the road somewhere around here," Welles said, poking at the map with his forefinger. "There's a hill about a mile behind the site where we should be able to get a good view of what's going on behind those fences from 400 feet above the harbor."

A few minutes later they passed the outskirts of La Trinitie on their left. Spruance caught a brief glimpse of the little town with its colorfully painted houses nestled along the improbably azure waters of the bay sparkling in the bright sunshine. Then the road curved back inland and around a hill, and the town vanished from his view.

Welles drove on for about a mile after passing the town before he pulled off to the side of the road. He consulted the map, and then pointed at a hill ahead and to the left. "That's where we want to go. There's the ruins of an 18th century chateau up there that looks right down over the bay. It should be an excellent place to observe the new facility without troubling our German friends. Let's just find a place to hide the car, in case anybody driving by gets curious."

A few yards further from the road at the base of the hill was a stand of scrubby trees and underbrush. Welles slowly drove the little car into the bushes. He and Spruance gathered up some of the branches the car had broken in its progress, and piled them on the trunk and rear bumper.

Welles stood back, hands on hips as he examined their work. "What do you think, Mr. Spruance?" he asked.

"Assuming that nobody is looking for us here, it will do," he answered. "It's good enough to keep casual passers-by from seeing it."

He took a leather knapsack from the back seat of the car and slid it over his shoulders, then followed Welles toward the path that ran up the hill. The trail meandered up the grassy slope between pitted boulders of volcanic rock. The incline was gentle at the bottom, but quickly became steeper as they went on. Although it was less than a mile from the car to the top of the hill, Spruance's calves were aching by the time they reached the ruined chateau.

Chateau Dubuc, Martinique

"This is the Chateau Dubuc, or what's left of it," Welles said, gesturing at the tumbledown gray stone walls on either side. "It was built around 1700, damaged in the earthquake in 1727, and abandoned about 1815. That wall is the remnant of the main house," he said, pointing to a tumbledown, undulating stone structure, which had obviously been part of a building at one time. It was perhaps twenty feet high at its highest point. "Why don't we climb up there and have a look?"

By picking their way carefully along the top of the ruined wall, the two men were able to reach the highest point of the structure. When they turned east and looked down, they were rewarded with a magnificent view of the town of La Trinitie on the other side of the bay and, more importantly, the new German port project.

Spruance straddled the wall, and slipped the straps of his knapsack off his shoulders. He laid the pack across his lap, and removed a large sketchpad, a ruler and a draftsman's pen with a fine nib. As he was unpacking, his companion was surveying the site through a pair of field glasses.

"Hamburg-America must have some big plans for Martinique," he commented. "Whoever planned this project was not thinking small."

By now Spruance had his own binoculars focused on the site. He was impressed by the scale of the development. He estimated that there were more than two hundred workers swarming over the new port. Massive quantities of dirt were being dug up by steam-shovels, moved about by heavy trucks and planed flat by bulldozers. He saw wooden forms that would require thousands of cubic feet of concrete to fill. "They have enough earth-moving equipment down there to build a medium-sized city. That big rectangular hole down by the shoreline on the left is the beginning of a dry dock, a big one. Why Hamburg-America would need something like that out here is a little hard to fathom."

"Do you think it will be big enough to handle a battleship?" Welles asked.

"Probably," Spruance said. He lowered the glasses, and began to sketch.

Three hours later, they were back in the yellow Citroen, on the road to Wilhelmshaven. The consul had been silent as Spruance filled the pad with sketches of the new facility, allowing him to concentrate on his work. The naval man remained uncommunicative as they returned to the car, appearing to be lost in thought. As they drove along, he reviewed the drawings he had made, flipping back and forth through the pages of the pad. Finally, he raised his head to look at Welles for a long time in silence.

"So, Mr. Spruance, after seeing the new facility with your own eyes, what is your professional opinion?" Welles asked.

He did not respond immediately. "I think," he said, after a considerable pause, "that if the Germans are serious about completing it, there will be a war."

CHAPTER THREE
WASHINGTON, D.C., APRIL 25, 1923

The 29th President of the United States, Frank Orren Lowden, smoothed his hair down for the tenth time in as many minutes, then sighed, his cheeks puffing out as he let out a long breath. He again examined the papers spread across his desk, as if hoping to find something other than what he had seen the first three times. Then he raised his head and looked all around the Oval Office, as if the solutions to his problems might be hidden in the dark green wallpaper or inscribed on the decorative moldings where the walls met the ceiling. His visitor waited patiently for the President to return to the business at hand.

The President fixed his gaze on the visitor. "Are you absolutely certain that we can rely on the accuracy of these drawings, General Wood?" he demanded.

"As I have already said, sir, I believe we can place our full faith in their accuracy..." Secretary of State Leonard Wood replied. The President raised his hand as if he was about to ask another question, so Wood hastily added, "...and can absolutely rely on the interpretations of them in the accompanying report from the Navy Department. The conclusion that the Germans are building a major naval base on Martinique is based on careful study of those sketches by our top naval experts, and I have no reason to doubt that the conclusion is correct."

He leaned forward over the President's desk. "These

shaded areas here will be runways for an aerodrome, and you can see where the frames of the airplane hangars have already been erected," he said, pointing out each feature in turn with his forefinger. "These thick arches extending out into the bay are submarine pens, or they will be. Over here is a tank farm for diesel fuel. And right here is a dry dock for..."

"I *know* what the report says, General Wood," President Lowden interrupted in exasperation. "I read it. I read the whole thing three times, as a matter of fact. Submarine pens! Aerodromes!" he exclaimed. He banged his meaty fist down on the desk. "God *damn* Woodrow Wilson, and your predecessor too, that sanctimonious 'Prince of Peace' Bryan. What were they thinking, allowing the Germans to acquire a colony in this hemisphere? Didn't they ever hear of the Monroe Doctrine?"

The Secretary of State patiently waited for the President's outburst to pass before responding. "If you will recall, Mr. President, Wilson was asked that very question right after he mediated the Treaty of Bryn Mawr..." this was the peace treaty that had ended the war between Germany and France in 1915, "...and his position at the time was that the Monroe Doctrine applied only in a case where a European power was attempting to colonize an independent nation in this hemisphere. Wilson said that it was never intended to be applied to a situation like this one, where an existing colony was simply being transferred from one colonial proprietor to another, as in the instance of Martinique. If you want my honest opinion, I might even admit that he had a pretty good argument for his interpretation. But suppose he *had* made an issue of it at the peace conference? What could he have done, exactly? Even if Wilson had asked, do you think this country would have been either ready or willing to go to war over a 400 square mile island in the Caribbean in 1915?"

The President ran his hand over his hair again. "No, I suppose not," he admitted, now speaking more calmly. "They sure left us with one hell of a mess, though. It would have served old Woody right if he had won the election. Then this baby would have landed exactly where it belongs: in his lap. No, I don't suppose the country would have been very eager to go to war with Germany, not in 1915, and not over Martinique. I wonder just how ready it is right now. I have a feeling the answer is 'not very.' But we can't sit around twiddling our thumbs and let the German Empire set up a naval base in the..." he paused. "Say, how far is that damned island from the Panama Canal?"

The same thought had occurred to the Secretary of State even before he had finished reading the report from the Navy Department, so he had consulted a map of the Caribbean before coming over to the White House, and he was ready with the answer. "A little over 1300 miles, sir."

"Not close, but too close," the President muttered. He suddenly sat up straight, and jabbed his finger at Wood. "I am counting on *you* to find a diplomatic solution to this crisis, General. The Germans will have to back down: they have no hope of winning if war breaks out. Anyway, the Kaiser would have to be insane go to war over *Martinique*, for God's sake."

Of course, by implication it would be equally irrational for us to declare war on Germany over Martinique, Wood reflected. He did not venture to share this thought with his superior, however. He said only, "I will do my best, Mr. President. There is one thing I must emphasize, sir. It is essential that we keep this under wraps as long as possible. Once it gets in the papers..."

Lowden nodded. "It will become impossible for the

Germans to back down without losing face, and there will be no lack of calls for war from some of the more irresponsible elements of the press here. I will issue the appropriate orders: no non-essential personnel to have access to this information, top secret, and so on."

"Thank you, Mr. President," Wood said. He rose, preparing to leave.

"I have every confidence you will find a way to resolve the crisis short of war," the President said, also standing, and extending his hand. "I chose you as Secretary of State because I thought you were the best man in the country for it, and I still believe that."

Wood stifled his urge to respond that perhaps the 300-odd delegates he released which gave Lowden the nomination at the 1920 Republican convention might have had something to do with it as well. He shook the proffered hand and said only, "Thank you, Mr. President. I hope I prove worthy of your trust."

Wood had been considering various approaches to handling the crisis before his meeting with the President, and he was already turning them over in his mind even before he left the Oval Office. Even so, as he walked back to his own office at the State, War and Navy Building, he did not share the President's confidence that a peaceful solution was very likely. He was afraid that the situation in Martinique might have already gone beyond the possibility of a diplomatic solution, and that the United States and the German Empire were already on the road to war.

CHAPTER FOUR
BERLIN, APRIL 28, 1923

The Secretary of State for the Colonial Office, his Excellency Gottlieb von Jagow, burst into the office of the Naval Minister, past the young Lieutenant who guarded the outer office as if he were not even present. After one look at the grim expression worn by the normally suave and imperturbable head of the *Reichskolonialamt*, the young man fell back and Jagow marched through into the inner office, and slammed the door shut behind.

"What is the meaning of this, Admiral?" he demanded angrily. He brandished a sheet of paper and thrust it at the Naval Minister. "We had agreed that there was to be no announcement until the base was ready to receive the fleet. The whole idea was to keep the project secret until it was too far along to be abandoned. You might have at least consulted with me before making an official announcement." He smoothed the paper, which he had unknowingly crumpled in his excitement, and read, "'The Ministry of the Navy is pleased to announce the construction of a modern naval base in the harbor of La Trinitie on the island of Martinique. When completed, this facility will be the future home port for the Imperial Caribbean Squadron.'"

Seated behind the desk was a huge man, dressed in the dark blue uniform of a Grand Admiral of the Imperial German Navy. His beard was long, white and forked, somewhat resembling a pair of fuzzy, inverted devil's horns, although there was nothing especially Satanic about his features. His name was Alfred von Tirpitz, and he was the father of the modern Imperial Navy.

Tirpitz reacted calmly to his uninvited visitor's anger, gesturing for him to take a chair. "Please sit, Your Excellency," he said. He waited for Jagow to settle himself before he went on. "I am sure you understand that sometimes events overtake the best-laid plans. There was no time for consultations or meetings: an immediate decision and instant action were required. A choice had to be made, and I made it. The Americans know all about the base."

"They *suspect*..." Jagow began.

"They *know*," Tirpitz interceded. "We have a source in the State Department who has confirmed that Secretary of State Wood met with President Lowden about the base three days ago. There was a complete report on the site with detailed sketches at the meeting. Lowden ordered Wood to find a diplomatic solution to halt construction. If action was not immediately taken to forestall him, he might have succeeded, to the ruin of our plans."

Jagow stroked the ends of his mustache thoughtfully, his earlier anger evaporated. "We were counting on presenting the Kaiser and the Chancellor with a *fait accompli*. It would be far more difficult for the Kaiser to concede to outside pressure if we could present him with the completed base. In the old days," he said in a wistful tone, "we would not have had to go behind the Kaiser's back with a project like this. He would have been all in favor of showing the world our strength. But since the war, all he cares about is developing the new lands in the East. He has completely lost interest in our overseas colonies.

"But," he added, returning to the present, "at least with

your official press release, the matter will be public enough that the pro-colonial papers will line up behind us and the Kaiser will face a storm of criticism in the press if he gives way to the Americans."

"And we know how much he loves reading stories like that," Tirpitz added. "I am glad you came over on your own, Excellency. I was about to ask you for a meeting to plot strategy. I expect we will be summoned by the All Highest to explain our little project..." he tapped the paper which Jagow had laid on his desk, "... before the day is out."

The meeting was held in the Imperial Cabinet Room. The room was embellished with gilt moldings along the ceilings, with oil portraits of former Imperial Ministers on the marble walls. The space was dominated by a long, highly polished mahogany table, which could accommodate at least thirty persons with ease. At the moment, however, only a handful of the elaborately carved Louis XIV chairs were occupied, all around the head of the table. On one side, his bulk overflowing his seat, was the Naval Minister, Admiral Tirpitz. Next to him, to his right, sat the dapper little Colonial Secretary, Jagow. Directly across from them were the Chancellor, Georg Michaelis, and the Minister of War, Crown Prince Rupprecht. Judging by their stony expressions, neither of the latter two men was particularly pleased to see their colleagues on the opposite side of the table. On the table at each place was a leather folder with the Imperial Seal embossed on the cover in gold. Behind the chair of each Minister hovered an aide, briefcase in hand.

Occupying the seat at the head of the table, naturally, was the Kaiser. The All Highest was particularly bad at concealing his emotions, having had little practice at the art. There was no need to guess what *he* was feeling, at least. Even the upturned points of the Imperial mustache seemed to quiver with indignation. Leaning forward in his seat, Wilhelm scowled fiercely at Tirpitz and Jagow. The Kaiser's folder was open, with a copy of the announcement released that morning by the Naval Ministry on top of the pile of papers.

"I am having difficulty deciding which of two courses to take," the Kaiser said, glaring at Jagow and Tirpitz, his eyes flashing dangerously. "Perhaps you gentlemen can advise me. I am uncertain whether I should simply demand your immediate resignations, or have both of you arrested and shot for treason. What are your thoughts on the matter, Jagow?" He fixed his glare on the Colonial Secretary.

The Colonial Secretary was a poor speaker at any time, but he was particularly tongue-tied in moments of stress and this was the most stressful moment in his recollection. He cleared his throat as if he was about to speak, opened his mouth, glanced at Tirpitz, then at the Kaiser, and finally said nothing.

"That is very sound advice, Your Excellency," the Kaiser said. He fixed the full force of his glower on the massive Admiral, who returned it with undiminished equanimity. "And what would my Naval Minister suggest I do?" he asked.

"I serve at Your Majesty's pleasure," Tirpitz replied. "If Your Majesty wants my resignation, a letter will be handed in by tomorrow morning. If Your Majesty wishes to arrest me, that is certainly his prerogative. I would not presume to advise him on the matter one way or the other. I can only say that I will remain Your Majesty's devoted and loyal subject, even when the blindfold is tied over my eyes and the order to shoot is given to the firing squad."

"You have an odd way of showing it," observed Chancellor Michaelis, who had been silent up to that moment.

"I for one have difficulty understanding how one so loyal and devoted to the Crown could engage in a conspiracy that may well involve us in a war with a major Power, without first taking the trouble to inform the Kaiser, or any *responsible...*" he pronounced this last word with caustic precision, "... members of the government beforehand, such as myself, or the Minister of War. At the minimum, I would have expected to see some mention of this new naval base in the budget, but I confess that at the moment I cannot recall any requests for funding this particular project."

In point of fact, funds for the new base had been requested under both the Naval and Colonial budgets, Jagow recalled uneasily. Of course, they would have been hard to find, as they had been included in (some might even say "hidden in") rather broad categories such as "harbor improvement and renovation" and "promotion of commercial development" in a way that some might consider deceptive, so he saw little purpose in bringing the matter to the Chancellor's attention.

Tirpitz remained both unabashed and unapologetic. "However the deed was done, the ultimate purpose was and remains a worthy one: the extension of the influence of Your Majesty's power, so that we may bring the benefits of German civilization to all the world."

"Those are noble aspirations indeed, Admiral," responded Prince Rupprecht dryly. "I am a little hard-pressed to see how becoming involved in a war we cannot win with the United States is likely to advance those particular goals, however."

The Kaiser now took up the thread, lifting a sheet of paper from the folder. "This Note came from the American embassy not two hours ago, an interesting coincidence, as I think you will agree." He paused, waiting to see if either of his

31

erring ministers would respond, then continued when they remained silent. "There are copies in front of you. Read it for yourselves, my loyal and devoted ministers," he said, the sarcastic lash of his final words making Jagow wince.

The Colonial Secretary quickly read over the American Note. He was surprised and relieved at the surprisingly moderate tone. "The Americans seem to be taking the news fairly well, under the circumstances. Secretary of State Wood expresses 'profound concern' that the new naval facility may result in 'a deterioration in the relationship between the United States and the German Empire,' but that is scarcely very belligerent language, all things considered," he said. "Moreover, he says that 'this Note should not be considered an ultimatum,' and that he is confident that we can reach a solution to our differences through peaceful negotiations. Based on this language, Your Majesty, there is no reason to believe that the Americans are contemplating war."

"True, the overall tone is quite moderate," Prince Rupprecht agreed. "On the other hand, Secretary Wood also suggests that the American solution would be for Germany to sell the colony of Martinique to them, 'to forestall any possibility of future friction over this issue,' and refers to negotiations only as to the price and details of the transfer, not as to the transfer itself, which does not appear to be subject to negotiation. I might also point out that the disclaimer '*this* Note should not be considered an ultimatum' might be taken to suggest that the *next* one may well be."

"The American Note was composed before your announcement this morning," the Chancellor said to the Naval Minister. "Had the matter not become public beforehand, the possibilities of reaching a settlement short of war would have been, needless to say, considerably greater. Now, however…"

"Now, however, we are left with little room for maneuver," the Kaiser cut in. "A settlement would look as if I had retreated in the face of American threats, and would seriously undermine our international prestige. I don't suppose that occurred to you, Admiral, when the Naval Ministry announced the building of the base and the formation of this new Caribbean Fleet?" The concluding question was delivered in a voice dripping with sarcasm.

The Admiral chose not to answer directly. "The Americans are not ready to go to war at this time, Your Majesty. More importantly, they will not be *willing* to go to war, especially over a small island in the Caribbean. I feel quite comfortable in predicting that if we are firm, it is the Americans who will give way. When they do, it will be a great triumph for Germany. No longer will other nations be able to disregard the position or interests of the German Empire in any future developments in the Western Hemisphere." He paused, and then added, "Of course, if Your Majesty has lost confidence in me, I shall resign immediately."

"And I as well, Your Majesty," Jagow chimed in.

Wilhelm shook his head. "Oh no, you're not getting off that easily. Sacking my two *loyal and devoted ministers*..." Again, Wilhelm's voice was redolent with ironic emphasis, "...would be equivalent to admitting that you had acted without my approval, and would signal to the world that I had lost control of my own government. I imagine you included that in your calculations when you launched this little scheme. You started this thing, and now you will see it through to the end. You may both go. Leave me, before I change my mind about the firing squad."

The men rose, bowed respectfully to their sovereign, and left the hall, their briefcase-carrying lackeys trailing in their wakes. The Kaiser glared at the backs of the departing ministers until the ornate doors to the cabinet chamber closed behind them. He turned to Chancellor Michaelis.

"Remind me again why I gave Jagow the Colonial Office," he said. "I know why I sacked him when he was in the Foreign Office: he was a miserable excuse for a Foreign Secretary. So why did I bring him back into the government again?"

"I seem to recall that the appointment was made as a sop to certain obstreperous colonial interests who were demanding a more aggressive policy in the overseas Empire," the Chancellor said. "After some debate, it was agreed…" (by which he meant that the Kaiser had decided to make the appointment against the Chancellor's advice) "…that it would be easier to give them a Colonial Secretary of their choice than to actually make any concessions on policy."

"Idiots!" Wilhelm grated. He slammed his open hand on the table. "These little islands in the middle of the ocean and trackless tropical jungles are useless, *worse* than useless, as they constantly threaten to drag us into wars with other Powers. Are these people too blind or too stupid to understand that the truly valuable land is all here in Europe, in our new acquisitions in Poland, the Ukraine, Belorussia and on the Baltic. That is where Germany's future lies, and that is where we should be investing our time and money, integrating our conquests in *Mitteleuropa* to forge a new Greater Germany, not in East Africa, Samoa and Martinique!"

Both the Chancellor and the Minister of War were so familiar with the Kaiser's oft-expressed views on this topic that they did not bother to respond. In any case, they were both in complete agreement with him concerning both the importance of new Central European acquisitions and the pointlessness of the overseas colonial empire.

"In my estimation, Jagow is merely a tool in this conspiracy," Prince Rupprecht said. "He would never have come up with such a complicated and risky scheme on his own. Tirpitz is the one I fear. The man is dangerous. He is afraid of nothing and will dare anything. Worse still, he is a hyper-patriot who truly believes that everything he does is, by definition, in the best interests of Germany."

"And that who anyone who opposes him is against Germany's interests, I agree," the Chancellor added. "What did the American, Pierce or Bierce, say? 'Patriotism is not the last refuge of the scoundrel, it is the first.' I might also point out that he is a very popular figure with the press, has a network of powerful friends in the naval lobby and a number of politically connected supporters both in and out of the Reichstag. Allowing him to retain the Naval Ministry after this Martinique business would obviously be dangerous, Your Majesty. On the other hand, dismissing him could touch off a firestorm of protest in the press and the Reichstag."

"As soon as this crisis that Tirpitz has manufactured is behind us," Wilhelm said slowly, "The Admiral will begin his long-delayed retirement." He paused. "I am still leaving the firing-squad option open."

The two Ministers began to smile. Then, seeing the Kaiser's expression, they became serious again. Nothing about the Emperor's tone or demeanor suggested that his final words had been a jest.

Kaiser Wilhelm II

CHAPTER FIVE
WASHINGTON, D.C., MAY 1, 1923

"So much for keeping the story out of the papers," President Lowden said ruefully. On his desk lay copies of the *Washington Herald*, the *Washington Daily News*, the *New York American* and the previous day's edition of the *Chicago Tribune*. "Have you found the source of the leak yet?"

"We just began the investigation, sir," answered Secretary of State Wood, who sat on the other side of the President's massive walnut desk. "We're not even positive that the story came from the State Department: it might have come from Navy, or even, dare I suggest it, from right here."

The President frowned. "I'd like to think I could rely on every employee in the White House who had access to the Navy Department report, General Wood." He turned to the third man in the Oval Office, his private secretary and political manager, who was seated to his left. "If I didn't trust you absolutely, Joseph, I might suspected that you gave the story to your little brother in Chicago." He picked up the *Chicago Tribune* to display the headline "War Clouds!", and smiled to indicate that he was joking.

The secretary, Joseph Medill McCormick, did not smile in return. "In that case," he said seriously, "I would have expected the *Tribune* to have broken the story first, rather than the Hearst papers."

He reached over to select the *New York American* from the pile, eyeing the copy of the Hearst newspaper syndicate newspaper dispassionately, like an entomologist examining a not particularly interesting insect specimen. The headline was thick, black and filled the entire news space in upper half of the front page: "Huns Threaten U.S.!" Below the fold, in smaller type, the subheading was: "Fleet Mobilized, Marines To Invade Martinique".

"Odd," President Lowden remarked. "I don't remember authorizing any such orders to the Navy Department? Did I send orders to the fleet, and simply forget, Joseph?""

"No, sir," McCormick replied. "That particular story may not be strictly based on reality. As we know, Mr. Hearst has never allowed the facts to limit his pursuit of a good story."

"His pursuit of greater circulation, you mean," Wood amplified. "Do you remember the reply he sent to Frederick Remington's telegram reporting that there was no war in Cuba? 'You furnish the pictures, I'll furnish the war.' He hasn't changed his methods since the Spanish-American War."

"On the positive side," the Secretary of State continued, "Scripps hasn't started beating the war drums, yet." The front page of the tabloid *Washington Daily News*, the outlet for the E.W. Scripps chain in the capital was comparatively undramatic: "Crisis In Caribbean", with a sub-heading "Secret German Naval Base In Martinique."

"Unfortunately, nobody much reads the *Daily News*, or the other Scripps papers, for that matter," McCormick observed gloomily. This was true. Of four newspapers in Washington, the *Daily News* had the lowest circulation, and this pattern was repeated over most of the big cities. The majority of the Scripps readers lived in rural areas and smaller cities in the Midwest, the South and the Southwest, and newspapers like the *Birmingham Post-Herald* did not have political influence to match the mighty *Chicago Tribune* or the big Hearst papers.

"The question is, with the story in the newspapers is it too late to cheat Hearst's readers out of exciting stories about big ships, big guns and big battles in the Atlantic for their entertainment over breakfast?" He looked expectantly at the Secretary of State, as did the President.

Wood pursed his lips. "As it happens, the leak to the press was irrelevant, since the German Naval Ministry released the story two days ago. I strongly suspect that release was a reaction to the Navy Department report on Martinique, which means that the Germans had a source inside our government."

"That doesn't make any sense," the President protested. "Why would the German government want to torpedo the chance for some kind of face-saving way out? Does the Kaiser want a war?"

"No, probably not, but perhaps someone else does," Wood answered. "Our embassy in Berlin keeps hearing unconfirmed rumors that this new base was not approved by Wilhelm and that a group in their Cabinet, possibly including the Naval Minister, Admiral Tirpitz, put this project together on their own initiative."

"That's incredible, if it's true," Lowden said. "But if it is true, why doesn't Wilhelm fire Tirpitz and his fellow plotters, and disavow this whole Martinique business?"

McCormick shook his head. "He can't without appearing to be incompetent. He would have to admit that his government was out of control. He'd look like a complete fool."

"Clearly the prospects for reaching a settlement with Germany have not been improved by the press coverage," Wood said. "And not just in this country. A large segment of the German press is behaving just as irresponsibly as our native warmongers, demanding that the Kaiser put down the pipsqueak democracy across the Atlantic. I think that we must prepare for the possibility of war, Mr. President, but I believe it is too soon to abandon hope of a peaceful resolution. I would prefer to keep direction of the nation's foreign policy in the hands of the United States government, instead of surrendering it to the likes of William Randolph Hearst."

"As far as your first suggestion goes, I have already ordered the Navy bring our fleet up to full operational status, and to concentrate the major units at San Juan, Puerto Rice, fueled, armed and prepared for combat," the President said. "Perhaps a show of force will help to persuade Wilhelm that we mean business. I agree with you about the second part as well, General. This is not the time to abandon our efforts to avoid an international conflagration: it is the time redouble our efforts to find a way to steer clear of the shoals of war. As you may have guessed, my office has been besieged with requests from members of Congress for a briefing on the Martinique situation. I have therefore requested that the two houses of Congress assemble in a joint session on Friday, May 4 at one o'clock when I will make a speech explaining the history of the crisis and the steps that are being taken by this government to meet it. I hope that by then I will have some favorable developments to report to them."

As Wood rose to depart, he silently reviewed the language of the German answer to his initial Note. "Under no circumstances will the Imperial Government engage in negotiations on the basis set forth [the sale of the colony to the United States]…" It was not the kind of response that seemed to offer much room for compromise. Rather than dampening the President's optimism by offering this gloomy appraisal to him, Wood simply said, "I sincerely share that hope, Mr. President," he said.

After Wood departed, President Lowden turned to his private secretary. "What do you think, Joseph? Do you think he can find a way out of this business without involving us in a war?"

When the two men were alone, McCormick dispensed with formalities. "I don't know about that, boss," he said, "but I can't believe that a war with Germany is going to make you more popular with the voters in the long run, in spite of all the patriotic fever Hearst, my brother and the rest the newspaper ghouls can stir up. How many Americans do you think are willing to risk their lives or the lives of their sons over a naval base in Martinique? How many do you think even know where Martinique is?"

"I would be willing to bet you twenty bucks that if you asked the average man on the street, eight out of ten of them would never have even heard of the place," the President said.

"No bet," McCormick said.

Lowden eyed him thoughtfully. "So what are you suggesting, Joseph? That it wouldn't be the end of the world if we let Wilhelm have his naval base in the Caribbean? What kind of political hay do you figure the Democrats could make out of that? They could claim that the German base fatally compromises the country's security. Would that hurt us very badly at the polls?"

"Maybe it would, and maybe it wouldn't," McCormick said judiciously. "Wilson went around telling everybody about his Nobel Peace Prize for negotiating the end to the war in 1915, and it seemed to go down well enough to get him a second term," he said, reminding the President of his predecessor's successful campaign in 1916.

"Look, boss," McCormick said, leaning closer and lowering his voice conspiratorially. "I'm not saying Martinique isn't important enough to risk a war over it, and I'm not saying it is. What I *am* saying is that you should at least consider all the alternatives *and* the political implications before you go down to the other end of Pennsylvania Avenue to ask for a declaration of war."

The President sat alone for a long time after McCormick left him, watching the afternoon turn to night and the streetlights on B Street flicker to life through the windows of the Oval Office. He trusted McCormick's political instincts, which was why he had chosen the man to run his campaign in 1920 and had made him his political alter ego after the election.

Certainly, his advice made sound political sense. There was a general election coming in eighteen months, and Lowden had every intention of winning a second term. If avoiding an unpopular war by conceding Martinique to the Kaiser would help him to retain the Presidency in 1924, should he not at least consider it? Any long-term evils the decision might lead to could be left for his successors to deal with.

On the other hand, he knew it would be irresponsible to kick the issue down the road, with the risk that the comparatively minor threat the German base would constitute right now might in a few years mushroom into a real danger to the country. No one was in a better position to appreciate this truth than he. Wilson had passed the Martinique mess along to him, and he resented it. He could not in good conscience do the same thing to whoever followed him in office.

More than his political future was at stake here. The long-term safety of the country might be imperiled if he chose to follow the easier course. If he allowed a potentially hostile foreign power to establish a permanent base in what had long been recognized as the United States' sphere of influence, what was to prevent Germany or others (Japan, for example) from doing the same thing again in the future? His choice, whatever it turned out to be, had major implications for the future of the country.

In the end, he made a characteristic decision. He would wait and see.

Office of The President of The United States, *c* **1920**

Leonard Wood 1903, an oil painting by John Singer Sargent

CHAPTER SIX
LONDON, MAY 2, 1923

Sir Edward Grey was a careful writer. He invariably prepared a fairly detailed rough draft to begin, and then refined the draft, often several times. His "drafts" could easily be mistaken for some other, less precise Foreign Secretary's final product.

For the present assignment, however, Grey thought that one draft, or two at the most, would suffice. He had been asked to ready an appreciation of the current crisis in the Caribbean for Prime Minister Churchill, as preparation for the discussion by the full Cabinet the next morning and for Question Time in the House of Commons in the afternoon.

The first section of the appreciation, a review of how the former French colony was acquired by Germany at the Bryn Mawr Peace Conference of 1915 that ended the Great European War, and the subsequent discovery that Germany was discovered to be building a major air and naval base in what had long been considered the exclusive preserve of the United States, was straightforward enough. In any case, the Prime Minister hardly needed Grey to remind him about it. At the time of the peace conference, when he was the First Lord of the Admiralty and before he had reached his position as the head of the government, Winston Churchill had gone about warning anyone who would stay in one place long enough to listen that the transfer of the island to Germany would lead to nothing but trouble.

The second section was Grey's summary of the possible outcomes of the crisis, including his guesses on the likelihood of each one occurring. Since there were not so very many possibilities (the Americans accepting the base, Germany withdrawing it, war), this section was comparatively easy to complete.

Characteristically, Grey declined to offer his estimation of the probabilities of the various resolutions of the crisis; long experience had taught him to be wary of making predictions on the record, and did so as infrequently as possible. He suspected that the longevity of his career as Foreign Secretary, now in its 18th year, was in part at least due to his discretion in making political predictions, or rather, in not making them.

It was the final section of the briefing that gave Grey reason to hesitate. This portion was intended for the Prime Minister's eyes only, and was not for consumption by rest of the Cabinet, let alone the House or the public. Mr. Churchill had asked for his Foreign Secretary's views on whether it would be in the interest of Great Britain to become involved in the crisis, and if so, what form that involvement should take.

This was a task that Grey would have gladly declined to undertake if he could have done so. The Prime Minister was a man who did not shy away from the prospect of war. Indeed, he sometimes seemed to relish it. He was reluctant to encourage his leader's belligerent instincts by offering advice that might encourage him to lead His Majesty's Government into a war that might be avoided. Grey hated war, considering it the greatest of all social ills.

On the other hand, as the Foreign Secretary, Grey's job was to guide the foreign policy of the British Empire down a path that served both its long- and short-term interests, and if that sometimes included the risk of war, then he was prepared to take that risk. In the years leading up to the Great War of 1914-1915, he had been one of the leaders of a small group in the Asquith Government who had worked to build stronger ties to France. In those years he had attempted, without success, to persuade His Majesty's Government to join a military alliance with Russia and France, in order to forestall German domination of the continent. Now, eight years later, looking at a Europe under the shadow of a victorious, arrogant German Empire, swollen with thousands of square miles of new territory and millions of new subjects, he saw his worst fears confirmed.

Should the British Empire take a hand in the crisis now shaping on the far side of the Atlantic? Realistically, if the Americans stood up to them, the Germans were in no position to do very much about it. It would be a naval war, with the High Seas Fleet thousands of miles from its bases, in an impossible logistical situation.

But suppose the American government, under a Progressive Republican President who had to date shown neither interest in nor knowledge of anything beyond the borders of his country, decided to back down and allow Germany to establish a naval and military presence only 1500 miles from Key West, and even closer than that to the vital Panama Canal? In Grey's view, such an outcome would pose almost as many dangers to British interests as to American ones.

From Martinique, the Germans would be in a position to interdict any shipping moving through the Caribbean, including traffic to and from the eastern side of the Canal. Moreover, with a base in the Caribbean Sea, in time of war the German Navy could disrupt shipping up and down the eastern coasts of both American continents with submarines, aircraft and surface vessels.

And there were other dangers as well. Since the war, Germany had become the unchallenged dominant Power on the Continent, and as such would be able to extort even more colonies in the Western Hemisphere (and elsewhere) from small neighbors with overseas empires whenever she wished. Denmark and Netherlands would be forced to cede anything the Germans wanted in the Americas, from the Danish East Indies, to Curacao and Dutch Guiana. The Dutch and Danes were in no position to resist German demands backed by the most powerful army in the world. Only Kaiser Wilhelm's often-expressed antipathy to the expansion of Germany's colonial empire had delayed this development, in Grey's opinion. But now, judging by the current crisis, it seemed that either the Kaiser had changed his mind about the value of overseas colonies, or had lost control of his government to the colonialists.

The time to stop Germany was now, Grey decided. It was better to risk involvement in a naval war in 1923, with the odds overwhelmingly on Britain's side, than to wait and give Germany a chance to expand its navy even further and build new bases for it all over the globe. By failing to join the coalition against Germany in 1914, Britain had ceded control of Europe to the German coalition. It was time for the British Empire to take a stand against the rising tide of Teutonic ambition; well past time, in Grey's opinion. Having made his mind up, he went to work, rapidly but neatly setting forth his recommendations to the Prime Minister.

CHAPTER SEVEN
BERLIN, MAY 2, 1923

The young Lieutenant in the outer office had announced him and then escorted him into the Naval Minister's inner office, but after he had been patiently standing in front of him for five minutes, Admiral Tirpitz had not glanced up, offered him a chair, or so much as acknowledged his existence.

Enough was enough, Reinhard Scheer decided at last. After all, he was an Admiral, the Chief of the Imperial Naval Staff, and was at the very minimum was entitled to the respect due to his rank from the old man, especially since he had made this call as a courtesy to Tirpitz. Still, along with his entire generation of fellow officers, Scheer held the Grand Admiral in such a high degree of reverence that he had difficulty overcoming the feeling that he was a young ensign being called on the carpet by his C.O. whenever he was in the Naval Minister's presence. Finally, he worked up enough courage to clear his throat.

Tirpitz did not look up from his reading. "What brings you here, Scheer?" he growled. When the younger man began to settle into a chair, Tirpitz said, "You don't need to sit down. You won't be staying that long."

"Grand Admiral," Scheer said nervously, "I have come to inform you that the Kaiser has commanded the Admiralty staff to prepare an assessment of the fleet's readiness for a naval war with the Americans."

"A complete waste of time," Tirpitz commented. "The

Americans are a race of soft, money-grubbing merchants, who care about nothing but their profits. They are degenerate and utterly lacking in the one essential virtue of the warrior: the willingness to place country above self. There will not be any war."

Scheer wondered if the *Grossadmiral* actually believed the nonsense he was spouting. Did he think that the grandsons of the men who had stormed Marye's Heights and Cemetery Ridge with such reckless courage in the American Civil War had degenerated into a race of cowardly milksops in just fifty years? Rather than allow himself to get sidetracked, he left the question unasked and returned to the purpose of his visit.

"Sir, the Americans are concentrating the principal combat elements of their fleet at San Juan, in their colony of Puerto Rico, only 700 kilometers from Martinique. They have…" Scheer began.

"So I have been informed," Tirpitz interrupted. "If you have come all the way over here to bring me that information, you have wasted your time. It means nothing. The Americans are merely posturing, putting on a show before they back down. They are not ready for a real war."

"The Admiralty was ordered to prepare an estimate of the combat capabilities of the American Navy, and to offer the Kaiser an assessment of the probable outcome of a fleet action against the Americans," Scheer continued doggedly. "Out of respect for your office and your person, I came to personally deliver a copy before…" he began, starting to open his briefcase.

"Never mind; I have already seen it," Tirpitz cut in again. He plucked the sheaf of papers from his desk and held them up for his visitor to see. "I was reading it when you arrived." He raised his head to look the younger man in the eye. "I consider this report to be unworthy of a German officer and a dereliction of your duty to the Fatherland. No true patriot would have written such a report."

At last, anger overcame Scheer's respect for and fear of his old superior. "You consider it a dereliction of my duty to tell my Supreme Commander the truth, that it would be a catastrophic blunder to send the High Seas Fleet to fight the Americans in the Caribbean?" he demanded, barely refraining from shouting. "For my part, I consider plotting behind your sovereign's back to involve the Fatherland in a war it cannot win worse than a mere dereliction of duty…" He clamped his mouth shut, curbing his final, bitter words.

"Did you want to say something more, Scheer?" Tirpitz prodded.

"Yes," Scheer answered. He spoke slowly, biting off each word. "I consider your actions in this affair, *Grossadmiral* Tirpitz, to be nothing short of treason." He spun on his heel, and marched out of the office.

Three hours later, Scheer was seated in the Imperial Cabinet Room, presenting the Admiralty report. In his customary place at the head of the table was Kaiser Wilhelm. On the right was the Chancellor Michaelis, while on the left sat Minister of War, Crown Prince Rupprecht and the Chief of the General Staff, General Wilhelm Groener. Standing directly behind each of these worthies was the inevitable briefcase-wielding aide. It was, in essence, a meeting of the Imperial War Cabinet, with the notable but understandable absence of the Naval Minister, and the somewhat more puzzling absence (to Scheer, at least) of Foreign Minister Arthur Zimmerman.

General Groener enlightened Scheer as to the cause of

Zimmerman's absence while they waited for the Kaiser to appear. It seemed that Chancellor Michaelis' investigation of the Martinique plotters within the government had turned up evidence against Zimmerman in the form of a memorandum from the Colonial Office to the Foreign Office. The memorandum proved that, at a minimum, the Foreign Secretary had been recruited by Jagow, and therefore had prior knowledge of the scheme. The Chancellor believed that Zimmerman had been an active member of the conspiracy, but could not find evidence to support this belief. In any case, Zimmerman had been dismissed from office and the Kaiser had asked Michaelis to temporarily wear a second hat as the Foreign Minister until the crisis was over.

"It would appear that my capital ships have sufficient range to reach the Caribbean with enough fuel remaining to maneuver and fight once they arrive, Admiral," Wilhelm said, frowning as he studied the charts of warship specifications Scheer had provided along with his memorandum. The Kaiser liked to speak of the Imperial Fleet as if it was a personal possession, like his Royal Yacht, the *Hohenzollern.* "I am not altogether clear on the basis for your pessimistic predictions. The *Nassau, Konig* and *Kaiser* classes all have a range of 15,000 kilometers, the *Heligoland*s 10,000, and the *Bayern*s over 9,000. The distance to Martinique is only 7,000 kilometers. Even my battle cruisers have the capability to cross the Atlantic. Is the United States Navy so overwhelmingly superior to my High Seas Fleet that you can foresee only disaster?"

"Your Majesty, if the battle was fought under equal conditions, in the North Sea, for example, I would have every confidence in the success of your navy," Scheer said earnestly. "But in this case, the conditions most emphatically would not be equal, but would be heavily weighted in favor of the

Americans. First, I ask you to consider the fact that the majority of your light cruisers lack the endurance to reach the Americas without refueling, as do all the torpedo boats and torpedo-boat destroyers. Without any screening or scouting capability, the big ships would be fatally handicapped, and vulnerable to enemy torpedo attacks."

The Kaiser looked unconvinced by this argument, so Scheer hurried on to stronger points. "But there is a more basic issue. The capital ships have sufficient range, Your Majesty is quite correct, *if* they are permitted to cruise at their most efficient speeds, which assumes that the Americans will allow them to make the crossing unmolested. We cannot assume this. But suppose that they do. Once our ships arrive on the far side of the Atlantic Ocean, what then? What if the Americans do not choose to engage in a fleet action immediately, but instead maneuver, looking for an advantageous moment to strike? If forced to make high-speed maneuvers to counter the Americans, your ships will quickly run out of fuel and will be helpless, as they will be far from any friendly port. We must assume that the Americans are as aware of this as we are."

The thoughtful expression on Wilhelm's face indicated to Scheer that the Kaiser was, if not wholly convinced, at least listening. By their grim faces, the Chancellor, the War Minister and the Chief of Staff already were in agreement with the Admiralty report, and needed no further persuasion.

"But even suppose the most favorable situation, that there is an engagement before a fuel shortage cripples the fleet?" the Admiral continued. "Even if your navy is victorious, it is most unlikely that the Americans will be utterly annihilated, just as it is most unlikely that the High Seas Fleet will emerge from the action without having suffered serious battle damage or critical depletion of its reserves of ammunition. The Americans can withdraw to their bases for repairs, refueling and rearming, and return, ready to renew the battle. How will your ships be re-supplied with fuel, shells and provisions? Where and how will the absolutely necessary repairs be made? The logistic situation is next to impossible."

The Kaiser grimaced.

"It is *possible*, if everything breaks perfectly in our favor, *if* the Americans charge headlong into an immediate fleet action, and are *if* they are obliterated in that battle, that German arms will prevail," Scheer concluded, "but the likelihood that your fleet will be first reduced to helplessness by lack of fuel, or by running out of ammunition, and then be destroyed *in toto*, is far greater."

"You are telling me that we cannot risk a naval war with the Americans in their back garden," Wilhelm said, sagging back in his chair. "You are telling me what I cannot do, but not what I can do. I am loath to give way so readily. I would like to test President Lowden's resolve but without provoking an outright war, as I have no intention of placing my fleet in the impossible situation Admiral Scheer describes. What do you suggest, gentlemen?"

"My advice remains the same as before, Your Majesty: I believe the wisest course would be to make a settlement with the Americans..." Seeing the Kaiser begin to cloud up, Chancellor Michaelis hastily went on, "...but if this still does not appeal to you, I think it may not be so difficult to arrange a test such as Your Majesty desires," he finished. He had been considering precisely this question since the beginning of the crisis, as he had never had the slightest faith in a military (or naval) solution. "We can at the very least discover whether the Americans are willing to accept the onus of starting the war upon themselves by firing the first shot."

Wilhelm leaned forward, his interest obviously piqued. "Pray continue, Chancellor Michaelis," he said.

Rupprecht, Crown Prince of Bavaria with his first wife, Duchess Marie Gabrielle *c* **1905**

War Ensign of the German Empire 1903-1919

CHAPTER EIGHT
WASHINGTON, D.C., MAY 4, 1923

At five o'clock, the President finally abandoned his attempts to get through the new Department of Labor employment report when he realized that he had just read the same paragraph three times and still did not remember a word of it. He knew that there were issues other than the crisis in the Caribbean that needed his attention, but for the moment he was unable to focus his full attention on anything else. His mind kept returning to the reception received by his speech to the joint session of Congress earlier in the afternoon.

As he walked up the stairs to the Capitol Building, he saw long lines of people waiting outside, still hoping for a chance to witness the speech. The address was being given in the chamber of the House of Representatives because it was considerably larger than the Senate chamber. The huge room was jammed to overflowing. The public and press galleries were packed with standing-room only crowds. In the diplomatic section every seat was occupied, as the representatives of foreign powers pressed in to hear America's response to Germany's challenge. Members of the majority Republican party spilled over into the aisle and invaded the Democratic side of the floor, much to the displeasure of the latter. The visitors from the Senate were given the front rows, while arrayed behind the President were the nine members of his cabinet, Vice President Warren Harding, Speaker of the House Frederick Gillett and president *pro tem* of the Senate

Albert Cummins.

The murmuring crowd fell silent when Lowden stood and somewhat diffidently approached the microphone atop its metal stand. At the urging of Joe McCormick, he had reluctantly allowed this to be the first Presidential speech to be broadcast to the nation through the relatively new medium of radio. "It's a chance to make your pitch directly to the public. There are over 600 radio stations out there now, with over 20 million people listening. If you can bring them around to your side, you'll be in a much stronger position with the Senate when the time comes to ask for a declaration of war," McCormick explained.

"*If* the time comes," Lowden corrected.

A technician from the radio station adjusted the height of the stand to place the flat metal disk of the microphone at the level of his mouth. "Just stand about six inches back from the microphone when you speak, Mr. President," the man advised. He then withdrew to an unobtrusive seat below the platform where his equipment was located.

Lowden eyed the device suspiciously, still wondering if broadcasting the speech on the radio had been such a good idea, then pushed all distractions aside, cleared his throat and began to speak. He did not have any written notes, nor did he need any. He prided himself on his ability to speak without notes. In twenty years of practice as a trial attorney before he had entered politics, he had never once used written notes to make either an opening or closing argument.

"The goal of the foreign policy United States under my predecessors has been to maintain peaceful relations with all the peoples of the world, and it is a policy that this Administration means to maintain." This had been greeted with loud cheers from the assembled legislators. Indeed, the applause from some of the Midwestern delegations had been almost hysterical.

"Our tradition has been to keep the peace by staying clear of the ancient dynastic squabbles of Europe, from which many of our ancestors fled to this continent. This tradition dates back to the very earliest days of our nation. George Washington in his farewell address warned, 'The great rule of conduct for us, in regard to foreign nations, is in extending our commercial relations, to have with them as little political connection as possible.' In his inaugural address, Thomas Jefferson counseled us to maintain '...peace, commerce, and honest friendship with all nations, entangling alliances with none', lest we be drawn into the endless and futile conflicts of the Old World." This, too, had met with overwhelming, clamorous approval both from the lawmakers seated on the House floor below him and the packed galleries above.

"But the United States has another ancient policy which guides our relations with other nations as well, a doctrine first expressed by another of our Founding Fathers, our fifth President, James Monroe, in 1823, one hundred years ago this year. Monroe made a solemn pledge that this nation would stand as the defender of our fellow free nations of this hemisphere and their people, a promise that we would place ourselves as a shield between them and the ancient enmities of the rival European empires. It is a promise that has never been broken during a century of challenges. The Monroe Doctrine is a necessary corollary to our policy of peace and non-involvement in the wars of Europe. For how can we avoid being drawn into the quarrels of the Old World if we allow it to bring those quarrels here, to the New? The enforcement of the Monroe Doctrine is not merely vital to our security, but in the long run is the surest way to guarantee peace for ourselves and our neighbors to the south." This was greeted with tepid approval at best; it was clearly not what the assemblage wanted to hear.

"We will spare no effort aimed at a peaceable resolution, nor reject any equitable proposal for compromise, nor fail to pursue any diplomatic initiative from any source to reconcile our differences and reach a pacific settlement of the present crisis in Martinique. Let there be no mistake about our peaceful intentions…" He paused, and there was another clamor of approval, and shrill cries from both the floor and the galleries of "*Peace! Peace!*"

He waited for the tumult to subside before he continued. "But neither should our resolve be misunderstood in Berlin. Let it be known that the United States will not tolerate the presence of a new naval base under the control of a foreign power in the Caribbean. We must not, we cannot and we will not stand idly by and permit the sea lanes to the Panama Canal or the republics of South and Central America fall under the shadow of the German Empire. We will redeem the promise of the Monroe Doctrine, and we will never retreat from that ancient policy, whatever the cost may be. And in the end, if all our labors to find a peaceful solution prove to be in vain, the Kaiser should know that we in this nation will not draw back from our historic duty, even if the fulfillment of that duty will require me on a future day to return here, to ask the advice and consent of the Senate for a declaration of war with the German Empire."

The response was surprising and dismaying. Lowden had not expected the suggestion of the possibility of war to be especially popular, but neither had he anticipated the vehement reaction he received. There was a tremendous commotion from the public galleries, booing, hissing and shouts of "*Peace!*

No! No war!" and the like. A few of the Senators applauded, nodding their approval, but most, along with the vast majority of their colleagues from the House of Representatives, sat in stony silence or shook their heads to indicate their disagreement with the sentiments he had expressed.

As President Lowden brooded in his office, reviewing the hostile reaction to his speech, a side door hidden under the green wallpaper, an entrance reserved for use by only the President and his private secretary, swung open and Joseph McCormick entered the Oval Office. He was returning from two hours of mingling with the legislators to get some sense of how Lowden's speech had been received by them. McCormick had been the junior Senator from Illinois before he joined his political fortunes to Lowden's, and was expert at taking the political pulse of the senior chamber.

"So, how bad is it, Joseph?" the President asked, after McCormick had settled into a chair. "Should I stop worrying about whether I have enough support on the Hill for a declaration of war and start counting the votes I'll need to beat impeachment?"

McCormick did not reply immediately to the question, which the President had intended facetiously. "Impeachment or trial?" he asked, gazing thoughtfully off into space for a moment, calculating. Then he shook his head, and said, "I wouldn't worry about it, boss; not a conviction, anyway. There's no way they could get 65 votes in the Senate."

"I am inspired by your confidence, Joseph," Lowden said dryly. "Now that my mind is relieved of that burden, I am free to devote my full attention to this Martinique situation. If push comes to shove, is anybody up on Capitol Hill prepared to vote for war with Germany?"

"You definitely can count on some votes from the

conservative wing of our party," McCormick replied. "Lodge..." (Henry Cabot Lodge, the senior Senator from Massachusetts) "... told me he had a dozen votes for war in his pocket, if and when you need them. And I think you can count on most of the Gulf Coast states. Somehow, Martinique doesn't seem so far away when your state includes Key West or New Orleans. I talked to Park Trammel..." (the senior Senator from Florida) "...and he said you can rely on getting the vote of every Senator from a Gulf Coast state. He said to tell you, 'The safety of the nation comes before party politics.'"

"It's nice to know the southern Democrats and New England will support me, but they're not enough, nowhere near enough," the President said. "What are the members of what is theoretically our Party about the possibility of war?"

"The situation could be better," McCormick admitted. "The Midwestern Senators are either pacifists or isolationists to a man, except for the ones who are both. Bob Lafollette..." (the senior Senator from Wisconsin) "...told me he that as far as he was concerned, Martinique wasn't worth the life of a single American boy, and that furthermore, if the Kaiser wanted to snap up every island in the Caribbean, including Bermuda, and annex them to the German Empire, he was welcome to them."

"Bermuda's not anywhere near the Caribbean," Lowden scowled. "It's off North Carolina, unless they moved it while I wasn't looking."

The private secretary chose to ignore this irrelevancy, and pushed on. "Lafollette speaks for most of the Progressive wing, and even the Senators who don't follow him will go along with him on the war issue. The Democrats aren't much better. The Democrats' populist Senators have no more interest in the Monroe Doctrine than our Progressives do. It's just a matter of time until Bryan opens his mouth, and that'll be the end of any chance to get any of the fence-sitting Demos from the West or Midwest. The farmers out there in Podunk still love the Boy Orator of the Platte, and everybody in his party is still afraid of crossing him."

"I'm surprised he hasn't already released a statement to the press condemning my war-mongering," the President said. "So to sum it up, the odds of getting Senate approval for a declaration of war are roughly equal to my chances of winning the National League batting title, is that about right?"

"You don't necessarily need a formal declaration to act, you know," McCormick pointed out. "As Commander in Chief you have considerable independent war powers under Article One, and plenty of recent precedents for it using them, too. Roosevelt, Taft and Wilson all committed either soldiers or sailors or both to foreign interventions, and none of them asked for Congressional approval."

Lowden shook his head. "You know better than that, Joseph. Ordering the Navy's battleships out to fight the German fleet is not the same thing as sending a few hundred Marines into Nicaragua, or even using a few thousand soldiers to chase bandits in Mexico. I cannot take a divided country into war, Joseph, I *will* not," he said. He paused, and then he sighed heavily. "The truth of the matter is, if I was still in the Senate, I would probably agree with Lafollette."

"I don't disagree with anything you're saying, boss. I was just reviewing all the options," McCormick said. "Maybe the diplomats will handle it, and you won't need to make that decision. What's the latest German response to our offer to negotiate?"

The President glanced up at the ornate clock that hung over the main entrance to the office. "I asked General Wood to come over for a briefing on developments at 5:30. He should be here shortly."

The two men fell silent, each lost in his own thoughts, until the intercom on the President's desk buzzed and the receptionist announced the arrival of the Secretary of State. After an abbreviated exchange of greetings, President Lowden immediately brought up the topic that was foremost in his mind.

"Has there been a German response to our new request for talks?" he asked. The expression on the Secretary of State's face told him the answer before he replied.

"No sir, Mr. President," Wood said. "They have not made any formal response through diplomatic channels. But they have answered indirectly."

He opened his briefcase, and drew out a few pages of paper. He handed one to the President and another to McCormick. "This is a copy of an official communiqué from the Chancellor's office that was released at noon today, Berlin time. You can see what they think of our proposals for talks over there."

" 'The Naval Ministry is pleased to announce that construction of the new naval facility at La Trinitie, Martinique will be placed on a new, accelerated schedule. The future home of the Imperial Caribbean Fleet is now expected to ready to receive units of the Imperial Navy by October 1 of this year. The first shipments under the new schedule will commence with the shipment of additional construction materials and equipment from Hamburg tomorrow'," the Secretary of State read aloud. "They didn't name the ships that will be doing the hauling, but they haven't made any secret of it either."

He read from another sheet he extracted from his briefcase. "Both of them are out of Hamburg: the *Orlanda*, which will be loaded with cement, and the *Ambria*, with a cargo of bulldozers and heavy trucks. Both ships are bound for Martinique."

"We seem to have our answer, then," McCormick said. "We ask for talks, and they speed up the construction."

"What the hell are they playing at over there?" Lowden demanded. "Does the Kaiser really want a war?"

"What I find particularly interesting about this communiqué is who issued it," the Secretary of State said thoughtfully. "The announcement is by the Naval Ministry, but the statement came out of the Chancellor's office."

"Say, that's right!" the President exclaimed. "What does that mean? Could it have something to do with the was a shake-up in Wilhelm's cabinet over this Martinique business that you told me about?"

"Yes sir," Wood replied. "Our people in Berlin say that the Naval Minister, Admiral Tirpitz, and the Colonial Secretary, Jagow, are in hot water over this affair. They confirm the accuracy of the rumor that the La Trinitie project was secretly formulated by a faction in the Cabinet headed by them, completely without the Kaiser's approval, and that he was hopping mad when he discovered it."

"I still have a difficult time understanding why Wilhelm doesn't climb down gracefully, instead of upping the ante," Lowden said, shaking his head.

"I have never gotten the impression that the Kaiser is a great one for climbing down, gracefully or otherwise, especially since he won the last war," McCormick answered for the Secretary of State.

Wood nodded in agreement. "Nobody likes to be publicly humiliated, Mr. President, and Kaiser Wilhelm likes it less than most. I would say that the Germans are not about to let us keep anything we aren't strong enough to hold for ourselves. I can't see them going to war over Martinique, but if we let them bluff us into backing down, they will be happy enough to take what we are unwilling to fight for."

The President looked back and forth at his advisors. "*You* tell me that there's not a chance in Hell that the Senate will support a declaration of war," he said, pointing at his private secretary, "and *you* tell me that if we don't at least make the Germans think we are ready to fight, they'll just mop the floor with us," he said to the Secretary of State. "So what am I supposed to do? The floor is open for suggestions."

"I have been considering an approach that might meet the needs of the moment, Mr. President," General Wood said. "It would involve the application of force, with a very small chance of it becoming lethal. We could effectively demonstrate the advantage of our position to the Germans, and bring the construction at La Trinitie to a halt at the same time. We would demonstrate to Germany and the world that we are strong and, best of all, the method is hallowed by custom and international law."

"If your idea is all that," Lowden said, nodding his head, "then yes, I think I *might* consider it," he said with heavy-handed irony.

"He's talking about a naval blockade of Martinique, sir," Joseph McCormick told the President. "Isn't that right, General Wood?"

"That is exactly right, Mr. McCormick," the Secretary of State replied. "A blockade is precisely what I am suggesting."

Lowden frowned. "I do not share your military background, General, so perhaps I have this wrong, but as I understand it, a blockade is an act of war and is only used between nations that are already at war. Would we not in effect be giving Germany a… what do you call it? A *casus belli* if we blockaded her colony in peacetime?"

"Actually, sir, we are on firm legal ground there," Wood said. "Back in 1827, a combined British, French and Russian force blockaded the Turks during the Greek War of Independence, at a time when none of the three blockading powers was at war with the Ottoman Empire. It was called a 'pacific' blockade."

"Unless I'm thinking about some other Greek War of Independence, that blockade did not end up peacefully," McCormick said.

"Well, eventually the Turkish fleet attempted to break through, and was destroyed at the Battle of Navarino," Wood admitted. "But the precedent is there. There was also the British blockade of New Granada in 1837, again in peacetime. That blockade resolved the dispute in that instance without a single drop of blood being shed. Since then, there have been more than a dozen such pacific blockades, none of which have resulted in a war. If the Germans choose to declare war, the blockade will not constitute a legal *casus belli*. Of course," Wood added, "that's no guarantee that they won't do it anyway."

Lowden nodded his head. "That's true enough," he agreed. "There are no guarantees of any kind in this business. You make the best decisions you can, and then you live with them. It's not as if we're talking about anything important, after all. It's only a question of war or peace, just the lives of thousands of young men." He leaned back in his chair, closed his eyes, took a deep breath and exhaled gustily.

"Gentlemen," the President said, "go get a cup of coffee, and return here…" he glanced up at the wall clock, "…at 7:00. I'll have a decision then."

Presidential address to Congress 1923

CHAPTER NINE
PHILADELPHIA, PENNSYLVANIA,
MAY 6, 1923

Just before he rapped his knuckles on the frosted glass of the Managing Editor's office door, Ray Swing remembered what John Curtis told him the day he accepted the post of Foreign Affairs editor at the *Philadelphia Inquirer*.

"My door will always be open to you," Curtis had promised. "You don't need to knock. When you want to talk to me, just come on in."

Swing shrugged and opened the door. The Managing Editor was on the phone. As Swing mumbled an apology for interrupting, Curtis shook his head and motioned vigorously for him to sit. Swing pulled up one of the battered wooden chairs in front of the editor's desk and waited patiently for the call to conclude. As far as Swing could tell (and he was doing his best not to listen very carefully), the editor was doing his best to fend off the importunate demands of a bookie, to whom he seemed to owe a substantial sum of money.

"Of course I'm good for it. I absolutely guarantee you'll have every cent by Thursday," Curtis said before replacing the telephone handset on the receiver. He looked at Swing, and shook his head ruefully. "All the trouble in this world comes from lack of trust. Just because I owe the fellow a measly few hundred…" he broke off.

"Sorry, I didn't mean to trouble you with my personal problems, Ray," he said. "What can I do for you?"

Swing laid two typed sheets of paper on the desk. "I'd like to run this on the editorial page tomorrow morning."

"I'll bet it's about Lowden's speech to Congress," Curtis said, as he gathered in the papers and began to scan them. Before Swing could respond, he went on, "I wish gambling on the nags was this easy."

"I told you when you came on board here as the Foreign Affairs Editor, you have *carte blanche* on international stories," Curtis said, as he continued to read Swing's piece, "and that includes access to the editorial page. I actually expected you to give me something yesterday, right after you got back from D.C. How was Lowden's speech, by the way?"

"I thought he made as good a case as possible, under the circumstances," Swing replied. "People don't know exactly what the Monroe Doctrine is, but they vaguely remember it from school and it sounds important. He certainly wouldn't have gotten very far explaining the *real* reasons we need to stand up to the Germans right now, even if it ends up in a war."

Curtis lowered the editorial, and looked at Swing quizzically. "Could you just remind me what those *real* reasons are again, Ray?"

Swing slipped his round, rimless glasses off his nose, polished them briefly with a handkerchief he retrieved from the breast pocket of his jacket, then resettled them on his face before he responded. "The German Empire is *big*, John," he said, leaning forward and speaking with great sincerity. "It is by all odds the greatest military power in the history of the world, and is more than capable of building a navy to match. The Kaiser ruled 80 million Germans in 1914, 80 million of the best educated, most productive people on the planet, and with the new territories Germany added in 1915 as a result of the war, the Empire now contains more than 130 million people. Germany dominates Europe today more thoroughly than any nation has since the days of Napoleon. And although she is quiet now, well, *was* quiet until this Martinique affair, Germany is not going to be content with what she has, John. She is still digesting the conquests in the Ukraine, Poland and on the Baltic, and welding those people into the Empire, but once that consolidation process is done, Germany will *use* that power. I was over there during the war, and I am convinced that the German government will *never* be satisfied with what it has; they will always want something more. You may have noticed how ruthlessly the Kaiser squeezed Emperor Charles on that so-called Free Trade Agreement, and Austria is his *ally*. It's only a matter of time until a new crisis comes up, and then..."

"O.K., O.K., you got me convinced, Ray," Curtis said, holding up a hand in token of surrender. "The Kaiser is the greatest menace to world peace since Attila the Hun." He looked at Swing shrewdly. "Still, you can't be too happy about being on the same side as Hearst, the *Chicago Tribune* and company."

Swing winced. "No, I'm not," he admitted. "If we lost 100,000 men in a war, but they sold an extra million papers, Hearst would be as happy as a pig in shit. Whenever people like that agree with me about anything, that's reason enough to reconsider my own position."

"So?" Curtis encouraged him.

"So, I have reconsidered, and I *still* think we have to give Lowden all the support we can," Swing said. "Just suppose we back down on Martinique. What happens when Wilhelm or his successor decides that he wants to add a few more islands to the German West Indies, say Curacao, or St. Thomas. Do you think the Dutch are going to say 'no' when big brother Germany asks to buy a colony or two from them? Or Denmark? Bismarck carved off a nice slice of territory from Denmark back in 1864, and I'm pretty sure the Danes haven't forgotten it. They'll be happy to give the Kaiser a few islands in the Caribbean, if that's the price of keeping his armies at home instead of marching into Jutland."

"So, you're saying that if we give in to Germany now, the issue will not go away," Curtis said.

"On the contrary, it will almost certainly return," Swing said, "and each time it does, it will be easier to surrender and more difficult and dangerous to stop. I hate war. No normal human being who has seen it for himself can feel any other way. But if this country is not willing to risk a small war now, as sure as God made little green apples, we will get a big one soon enough."

"All right," Curtis said. He scribbled something on the editorial. "This will run in tomorrow's edition. Is there anything else?"

"Yes," Swing answered. "I think it's about time I put the 'foreign' back in foreign correspondent again. I want to take a long trip through the New German Empire in Eastern Europe, and file a series of stories from over there. I've been reading up on how they are making German the official language in Poland, the Ukraine, Lithuania, and so on, and outlawing the teaching of the native languages. The authorities in Berlin are also doing everything else they can to Germanize their new subjects, including locking up anybody who speaks or writes in favor of local autonomy or ethnic rights within the Empire. I think if people hear what the Germans are doing to their subject peoples over there, it might just open some eyes in this country."

"O.K., fine," Curtis said. "Just give me a rough idea of your itinerary and approximate expenses in advance. When do you think you'll be going?"

Swing rose from the chair, preparatory to leaving the editor's office. "Well, that's not really up to me, is it, boss? It's pretty much in the hands of Lowden and Kaiser Wilhelm." He turned and left, closing the door behind him.

The Philadelphia Daily News Building, formerly The Everson
Building. Built for The Philadelphia Enquirer in 1923

CHAPTER TEN
OFF MARTINIQUE, MAY 16, 1923

When the call to the bridge came, Captain Claude Bloch was at his desk, catching up on his paperwork, writing efficiency reports of the officers serving under him in the Second Division of the Martinique Interdiction Task Force. Bloch's Second Division consisted of eight destroyers divided into two squadrons, and two cruisers (so-called under the new terminology, formerly "second-class cruisers"), *Milwaukee* and *St. Louis*. Bloch was flying his flag in *St. Louis*, while the entire Interdiction Force was under the command of Rear Admiral Thomas Hart in the battleship *North Dakota*.

The Task Force had been patrolling off Martinique for eight days. In that time, Bloch's command had stopped two ocean liners filled with French tourists, several coasters working the Antilles chain from the Windward Islands up to Key West and back, and a *maru* out of Yokohama via the Panama Canal stuffed with cheap Japanese trade goods. None of these vessels was carrying any of the heavy construction materials or machinery that were on the banned list. Since almost nothing of consequence had happened since the Task Force had taken up station covering the shipping lanes to the island, Bloch was finding it difficult to say much on the forms concerning the performance of his officers other than "Lieutenant Commander _____... " (or "Commander_____..." or "Lieutenant_____...") "...has handled his assigned duties adequately."

Although Bloch's destroyers were comparatively up to date, all having been built in 1917 or later, his cruisers were, to put it politely, nearing the end of their useful service life or, to put it more bluntly, were about ready for the scrap yard. Both *Milwaukee* and *St. Louis* had been launched in 1905, and everything about them, from the outmoded coal-burning, triple-expansion, reciprocating engines (newer warships had the more powerful and efficient diesel-turbine engines), to the outmoded placement of the main batteries in swivel mounts along the hull (as opposed to the modern system where the guns were grouped in centerline turrets), showed the age of the two ships. The design was obsolete; it had been obsolete even before the keels of the ships had even been laid down. In point of fact, the entire class of warship to which *St. Louis* and *Milwaukee* belonged was obsolete: no first-class navy had built protected cruisers for at least 15 years. The United States Navy boasted battleships and destroyers that were as good as those in any navy in the world, but as yet it had no modern cruisers to match them.

On the other hand, the old girls were more than good enough for this blockade (no, we're calling it an "interdiction", Bloch mentally corrected himself). *St. Louis* and *Milwaukee* both were capable of twenty-two knot speeds for at least a short time, which was fast enough to run down any freighter ever built, and with their fourteen six-inch naval rifles, they could not only catch their quarry if it fled but also, if necessary, sink it with ease.

As the metal risers of the ladder squeaked under his weight as he ascended to the bridge, Bloch reflected that mere age did not necessarily mean that a ship was ready for the breaker's yard, or a man either, for that matter. Bloch had joined the Navy back in 1899, six years before his two cruisers had been commissioned, and he personally felt far from obsolescent and not the least bit ready for the scrap heap.

The Captain of *St. Louis*, Commander William Leahy, was on the bridge when Bloch arrived. He would have been surprised if Leahy had not been there before him; during their relatively brief association, Bloch had gotten the impression that Leahy made a habit of being in the right place at the right time. "What is the situation, Captain?" he asked (the officer in command of the ship is always addressed as "Captain" while on board, even if his actual rank is lower). "Have we spotted our pigeons?"

"Sir, Commander Halsey, DesRon Two..." (Lt. Commander William Halsey, who was in command of the four destroyers that comprised Destroyer Squadron 2) "...reports two freighters flying the German flag, bearing one-eight-six, at a speed of ten knots," Leahy answered. He pointed. "You can just about make out their smoke on the horizon, Commodore." (As there could be only one Captain, that is, one commanding officer on a ship, an officer who held the *rank* of Captain, like Bloch, had to be addressed by the courtesy rank of "Commodore".)

Bloch aimed his field glasses in the direction Leahy indicated, and was rewarded with the sight of two faint plumes off to the northeast.

Leahy continued. "The ships have not been identified as yet, but..." He broke off as a messenger from the radio room rushed onto the bridge and saluted.

"Sir," he said, extending a paper to Leahy, "the radioman just transcribed this message."

Leahy took the folded sheet and handed it on the Bloch, who opened it and scanned the contents. "It's from Halsey," he said. "The ships have been positively identified as *Orlanda* and *Ambria*, out of Hamburg. They're the ones we've been waiting for."

Bloch gestured to a waiting sailor. "Take down a message to Admiral Hart: 'At approximately 09:12 hours freighters *Orlanda* and *Ambria* sighted, heading 186, approximately 45 miles northeast of Basse Pointe…'" (the northeastern corner of Martinique) "… presumed destination La Trinitie. Vessels will be stopped and searched per standing orders.' Get that over to the radio room on the double," he said.

Leahy was issuing orders at the same time. "Sound general quarters." He continued over the sudden din of bells and the slap of running feet on the metal deck. "Helm, steer course zero-one-zero, all engines at one-half."

Bloch raised his field glasses again, following Halsey's destroyers as they attempted to stop and board the two German merchantmen. The process was taking longer than usual.

Until today, all of the Martinique-bound ships had responded promptly to radio requests from the Task Force to stop and allow naval personnel to board and inspect them. The presence of all those guns tended to make the typical merchant captain understandably nervous. But the skippers of *Orlanda* and *Ambria* seemed to be less impressionable than their colleagues. The destroyers ordered the two vessels to "stop engines and prepare to be boarded", first with semaphore flags, then in Morse code with Aldis lamps, but the German freighters continued to plow stolidly ahead as if the American destroyers flanking them did not exist.

Commander Leahy watched the slow-motion chase with growing amazement. "What do those two clowns think they're doing?" he demanded. His next remark made it clear that the "two clowns" to whom he referred were the captains of the

German ships. "Do they think they're going to outrun four *Wickes*-class destroyers? Neither of those tubs could make fifteen knots if you threw them off the 12th floor of the Dixie Hotel," he said, disgusted at the inexplicable stupidity of the German captains.

Bloch suppressed a splutter of laughter at his subordinate's outrage. "They know exactly what they're doing, Bill," he said, his field glasses still raised to his eyes. "They don't think they can get away from 35-knot destroyers. They're just playing the game out to the last move, exactly the way their bosses in Berlin want them to. There," he said, "Halsey is tired of horsing around."

The latter remark was prompted by a pair of sharp reports. Two of the destroyers had fired four-inch shells across the bows of the German ships. The obvious implication was that the next two shots would not be warnings. The freighters slowed and came to a dead stop in the glassy smooth seas, as a destroyer approached each, and tied up alongside.

"I see," Leahy said. "They just wanted to know if we're serious about this interdiction."

"I think they knew that well enough, Bill," Bloch said. "A lot of this business is just a little drama to establish a legal position for the record, and I predict that the show is far from over."

They watched and waited as boarding parties went aboard the freighters. Twenty minutes later, another message came in from the radio room. Bloch read it.

"It's from the *Mahan*..." (Halsey's flagship) Bloch said. "Captains Lutjens and Marschall do not consent to inspections of cargo. Will not voluntarily allow review of cargo manifests. Demand audience with chief of 'pirates' who have detained them."

Bloch looked at the young sailor who had brought the message from the radio room. "Take down a reply to Commander Halsey, son." He waited as the young sailor whipped a small pad of paper and a pencil from his pocket. "Send merchant captains to *St. Louis* by fastest available motor launch. Pirate chief will grant them an interview." He surveyed the bridge crew with his eyebrows raised in mock surprise at the ensuing snorts of laughter.

Forty minutes later, the two German captains were escorted into the wardroom of the *St. Louis*. Bloch was seated at the dining table, cradling a cup of coffee.

Captain Gunther Lutjens had short, light brown hair, light blue eyes and a slender build, while his colleague, Captain Wilhelm Marschall was shorter and stockier, had darker hair and brown eyes. From the moment they entered the room, Bloch saw by the way they carried themselves that these two men were no more merchant captains than they were ballet dancers. He had no doubt that both were veteran officers in the *Kaiserliche Marine*, the Imperial German Navy.

Nor was he surprised. Certainly, if he had been in charge of the operation from the German side, Bloch would never have assigned such a job to civilian captains. The part played by the skippers of the two freighters was an important one, requiring nerve and intelligence, a role that required officers to remain calm when confronted by hostile warships and gunfire. Not many merchant captains were prepared for that kind of work. Bloch could see by their faces that both of *these* men were ready to carry out their orders at all hazards, even at the risk of having their ships shot out from under them.

He rose. "Captain Lutjens, Captain Marschall, please make yourselves comfortable," he said. "Would you like some coffee?"

The interpreters assigned to the Germans immediately began to translate. Before they got out more than a few words, however, Lutjens interrupted. "We will communicate in English. We do not require interpreters." His English was accented but perfectly understandable. Lutjens looked at his companion, who nodded in agreement.

"Fine," Bloch said. "You interpreters are dismissed." He returned his attention to his visitors. "Now, do either of you want…"

"We do not require refreshment, Captain, and we are quite comfortable standing," Lutjens said harshly.

"Suit yourselves, gentlemen" Bloch shrugged, resumed his chair and took a sip from his coffee cup. "You wanted to see me. What would you like to talk about?"

"I should think that would be obvious," Marschall said, speaking for the first time. "We demand to know why you believe that the American Navy have the right to stop and board a German ship, carrying German goods, from Germany, to a German possession in the German Empire. Your actions, Captain Bloch, are nothing short of piracy."

"That does not even include the most provocative act of all: firing on ships of the Imperial Merchant Service while engaged in official business," Lutjens added.

"So you admit you are acting on orders from your government," Bloch said.

"We admit nothing of the kind," Lutjens answered. "Neither our cargos nor our orders are your concern. Rather than worrying about them, you should be concerned about the consequences of your blatant violation of international maritime law."

Bloch suppressed at smile at the German's simulated

show of outrage. It was apparent to him that Lutjens was in complete control of his emotions, as cool as a riverboat gambler betting his entire pile on a busted flush.

"I hope our actions are a great deal short of piracy. We do not intend to take or damage any of your cargo. We have no intention of interfering with your ships any more than is absolutely necessary, Captain," Bloch said. "You have your orders and I have mine, and I intend to carry mine out. At the moment, the island of Martinique is under a limited interdiction by order of the President of the United States. Until further notice, no construction materials or equipment may be unloaded there." He extended a sheet of paper with a typewritten list of the banned items under the interdiction. Lutjens made no move to take it.

"This is the list of interdicted goods," Bloch said. "Once we have inspected your ships, and are certain that you are not carrying anything on this list, you will be free to continue on to Fort-de-France…"

"The name of the city is *Wilhelmshaven*. It was renamed in honor of the Emperor in 1916," Marschall interrupted, genuine annoyance apparent in his voice.

"Oh yes, of course, my mistake," said Bloch apologetically. He had intentionally called the colonial capital by its old name to provoke precisely this reaction from his adversary. The Germans were particularly sensitive to anything that appeared to be disrespectful to their Empire or to the Kaiser. Bloch hoped that one of the bogus merchant captains might get angry enough to say or do something foolish.

Lutjens shot a look at his colleague, and Marschall subsided. "As you have no right to stop our ships, you have no right to inspect our cargo, Captain Bloch," he said. "What do you intend to do if we proceed to Martinique, as is our legal right?"

"In that case, Captain, if I were you I would make absolutely certain that your crews are familiar with their lifeboat drill," Bloch answered, "because I can assure you that without that inspection, neither *Orlanda* nor *Ambria* will ever get any closer to Martinique than they are right at this moment. If you force my hand, I will sink both your ships." He studied the faces of the two Germans, who returned his look impassively. "I would strongly advise you to take this warning seriously."

"On the other hand," Bloch continued, "if you refuse to allow us to carry out an inspection, you may feel free to offload anywhere other than Martinique. Castries on St. Lucia has an excellent deep-water harbor, and…"

"We did not come here to ask your advice, nor do we want it," Lutjens snapped. He scowled. "Under the circumstances, we have no choice but to submit to your illegal actions. This is not the end of this affair. Please have us returned to our ships immediately." He spun on his heel and, followed by his colleague, he marched out of the wardroom.

From the bridge, Bloch watched through his field glasses as the German freighters turned and lumbered off together in the general direction of Dominica, the next island north of Martinique in the Antilles chain. They were seen on their way by the four destroyers of DesRon Two.

Leahy, who was standing at his side, asked quietly, "So, what do you think, Claude? Is that the end of it?"

Bloch did not answer immediately. "I don't know, Bill," he said at last. "Logic tells me that the game is over, but Lutjens didn't act like a man who was ready to throw in the towel. He reminded me of something from when I was in grammar school."

"Oh?" Leahy asked. "What was that?"

"He put me in mind," Bloch said, lowering the binoculars, "of a kid who just got pushed around by the schoolyard bully and was going back home to fetch his big brother."

USS St. Louis

USS Mahan

CHAPTER ELEVEN
BERLIN, MAY 18, 1923

Admiral Reinhard Scheer had been summoned to another meeting of the War Cabinet. The subject under discussion was almost certainly going to be the response to the American blockade of Martinique. Scheer had a very strong premonition that he was not going to be very happy with the outcome of this meeting.

He entered the great hall followed by his aide, and took his seat at the long conference table next to the Minister of War, Crown Prince Rupprecht. Normally, this would be the place reserved for the Naval Minister, but under the current circumstances, Admiral Tirpitz was not welcome in the Cabinet Room. Scheer was, for all intents and purposes, the acting Naval Minister. It was an additional responsibility he would happily have done without.

The assembled Cabinet Ministers (and Scheer), all rose to their feet when the Kaiser entered. Wilhelm waved them down again impatiently as he allowed an aide to seat him.

"There is no time for nonsense," he said. "The time has come to act, and to act decisively." He gestured theatrically.

"The Americans have fired on our ships. Our Captain Lutjens reports that they would have sunk them if they had not turned back," he said. He glared at his Chancellor accusingly. "Did you not tell me, Michaelis, that the Americans would not dare to fire on our ships for fear of starting a war?"

In fact, he had never said anything remotely like it. "I

merely said, Your Majesty, that they might be reluctant to use force in this situation, as President Lowden does not appear to have very strong support for his Martinique policy. If you recall, I also suggested that if the Americans held firm, we would ultimately either be forced to negotiate from an even weaker position than before, or else escalate the situation in a very dangerous manner. I must strongly advise Your Majesty against the latter course."

The Chancellor remained outwardly impassive under the continued glower of his sovereign, so Wilhelm turned to his Minister of War. "And are you in agreement with the Chancellor, Rupprecht? Do I have no choice but to surrender to the Americans, to humble Germany and myself before the *democracy*..." This last word emerged dripping with contempt and vitriol, "... without a single blow being struck in defense of my honor?"

The Crown Prince of Bavaria smoothed his mustache thoughtfully with his thumb and forefinger before responding. "I think, Your Majesty, that the inherent risks of escalation outweigh the possible gains," he said judiciously. "Certainly, if we are forced to come to terms with the United States, there may be unflattering articles in the press and some slight, temporary diminution of our prestige overseas for a time, but memories are short and such things will soon pass without causing any permanent injury to our international position or your reputation."

This was obviously not the response Wilhelm wanted. He showed his displeasure by clenching his right hand, which rested on the table, in a fist, and scowling more ferociously than ever. The Kaiser was silent for a long time, as he tried to regain control of his temper. His complexion, which had been flushed with anger, slowly returned to normal.

"Admiral Scheer," he said, "which of our battleships has the greatest ability to absorb battle damage? In other words, which ship, if placed in a hopeless fight, would give its crew the best chance to survive?"

Scheer was taken aback by the question. Was the Kaiser planning to sacrifice one of his dreadnoughts? "Does Your Majesty wish me to consider the issues of firepower or speed?" he asked, to gain time to think.

"No, they would not be relevant for my purposes. I am just interested in ability to survive punishment," Wilhelm answered.

"In that case," Scheer said, "I would probably choose one of the *Nassau* class, Your Majesty. The principal differences between the *Nassau*s and our later battleships are in propulsion and armament. The *Helgoland* class and all subsequent types have 30.5 centimeter main batteries, or larger, and are turbine powered. *Nassau* and her sisters have 28 centimeter main guns, and triple-expansion engines. But the *Nassau*s all have extensive watertight compartmentation and double hulls precisely like the later dreadnoughts, and they are as tough to sink as any capital ships afloat."

"Ah, Admiral Scheer," Prince Rupprecht said, "Unless I am mistaken, I seem to recall that *Pommern* was lost at the Battle of Cape Cepet. Wasn't she a *Nassau* class dreadnought?" Rupprecht was recalling the 1915 sea battle off Toulon, where the French fleet had been virtually annihilated at the cost of a single German battleship.

"You remember correctly, Your Excellency," Scheer said. "No ship is unsinkable, if she is holed badly enough below the waterline. There are no guarantees. But, I repeat," he continued doggedly, "I do not know of any capital ship afloat today that is more capable of surviving battle damage than the

Nassau class."

The room fell silent again. Suddenly the Kaiser thumped his fist on the table. "I will see Americans in Hell before I bow my head to them," he said. "Admiral Scheer, which of the *Nassau*s is closest to operational readiness?"

"I cannot answer that question at this moment, Your Majesty," Scheer said, "but I will certainly have an answer for you by..." he glanced at the elaborate gilded wall clock over the Kaiser's chair, "1600 hours today."

"Whichever one it is will be ordered to proceed to Dominica at the earliest possible date, to rendezvous with our merchant ships, *Orlanda* and... what's the name of the other one?" Wilhelm asked.

"*Ambria*, Your Majesty," Michaelis supplied the name.

"Yes... with *Orlanda* and *Ambria,* and to escort them to the harbor at La Trinitie, Martinique," the Kaiser continued. "If our ship encounters American battleships, her Captain is not to fire her guns at the Americans *under any circumstances...*" He paused and stared at Scheer to emphasize the importance of this point.

"Not even in self-defense, Your Majesty?" Scheer asked, aghast at the thought.

"*Under no circumstances*, Admiral, is our battleship to fire on the Americans," the Kaiser repeated. "The Captain will be under orders to surrender the ship or abandon it, if necessary, if the damage is too serious, but he must *not* discharge his weapons at the Americans. Is that understood?"

"Yes, Your Majesty," Scheer said unhappily. "But may I be permitted to ask why?"

"Do you understand, Michaelis?" Wilhelm asked, turning to his Chancellor. He immediately answered his own question. "Of course you do. Please explain to Admiral Scheer."

"We are in no position to go to war, Admiral," the Chancellor said, "but the Kaiser does not believe that the Americans will fire upon a ship of the High Seas Fleet at the risk of precipitating a war themselves. If they do, then we will concede the game in Martinique..." He turned to look at his monarch, who made a sour face but nodded his agreement. "...and accept American shellfire without returning it, so as to give no excuse for a declaration of war."

Scheer must have still looked puzzled. "Do you know the game of poker, Admiral?" asked Prince Rupprecht.

"I don't play it myself, but yes, I know the game," Scheer answered.

"What the Kaiser is planning is essentially a 'bluff' – an attempt to win the pot with a weak hand, by pretending to have a strong one," the Minister of War explained. "If the Americans call our bluff, we shall have to throw in our hand, at the possible cost of a dreadnought battleship and its crew."

"I see. That is why Your Majesty wanted to know which ship could survive the greatest amount of damage," Scheer said, understanding at last. "I must get back to my headquarters immediately. If Your Majesty will excuse me..."

"You are excused, Admiral Scheer," the Kaiser said.

As Scheer's footsteps echoed in the great hall, Wilhelm turned back to his Ministers. He looked them over. "I see that you do not approve of my stroke," he said. "But sometimes great things can be accomplished only by taking great risks."

Crown Prince Rupprecht remembered his governess reading him an old fairy tale about a little girl and a fox when he was a small boy in Bavaria. Unconsciously, he murmured a line from the story under his breath. "Be bold, be bold... but not too bold."

"Did you say something, Rupprecht?" Wilhelm asked.

"Oh, nothing, Your Majesty," he answered. "Nothing of the slightest importance."

Broadside from a battleship _c_ 1920

CHAPTER TWELVE
LONDON, MAY 19, 1923

At the request of the Prime Minister, Sir Edward Grey stayed behind at Number 10 Downing Street after the cabinet meeting had concluded.

"I never had the opportunity to tell you my opinion of your memorandum on the Martinique situation, Edward," the P.M. said. "If the Americans had not stood up to the Kaiser, I would have followed your recommendations. You set out the issues with striking cogency, I think. Fortunately, it does not appear that we will be obliged to take any part in the matter. It seems to be all but settled."

"Then you are quite certain that the Germans have completely given up on the project, Winston?" Grey asked.

A look of mild puzzlement crossed Churchill's face. "Do you have any reason to suspect they have not? Some new intelligence, perhaps?" he asked.

Grey shook his head. "Nothing specific that I can put my finger on, no. It is simply a feeling..." the Foreign Secretary trailed off.

"A feeling, yes?" Churchill prompted.

"It is just not like Wilhelm to give way so easily in a crisis. Generally, that doesn't happen until the situation is on the verge of a catastrophe," Grey explained. He tried to make light of it. "More than likely it is nothing more than a bad piece of fish from lunch."

"As you know, the Grand Fleet has been on 'maneuvers'

for the last two weeks, in the event that President Lowden was unable to resolve the crisis on his own, and the fleet was needed immediately," the Prime Minister said. "I was considering ordering Admiral Beatty to stand down after the recent news from America, but perhaps it would be better to wait a little while longer, until we are absolutely certain that the crisis is over. What are your thoughts, Edward?"

Grey nodded. "I agree, Winston. In the next week we will either see the Germans open negotiations for a peaceful settlement with the Americans, or..." Again, the Foreign Secretary paused, leaving the thought unfinished.

This time the Prime Minister finished for him. "...or they won't," he said grimly. "We'll keep the fleet on maneuvers for now."

CHAPTER THIRTEEN
WASHINGTON, D.C., MAY 22, 1923

"They're sending a *battleship* over here?" the President demanded in voice that combined outrage with disbelief. Before him on his desk lay a copy of the latest announcement from the office of the Chancellor in Berlin to the effect that the dreadnought *Rheinland* was being dispatched to the Caribbean to escort the merchant vessels *Ambria* and *Orlanda* to their destination in Martinique.

Lowden glared at his Secretary of State accusingly. "It doesn't look like our blockade... excuse me, our 'interdiction'... is going to remain 'pacific' for much longer, does it, General?" he asked sarcastically.

Wood's expression did not betray any emotion, but his tone was icy. "Mister President," he said, "if you believe I have mishandled this crisis, you only need to say so directly and my letter of resignation will be on your desk before the close of business today."

The President's face clouded in anger. Before he could say anything that might create an irreparable breach with the proud Wood, his private secretary, Joseph McCormick, jumped in. He knew that Wood's resignation at this point in the growing crisis would be a political disaster of the first magnitude. "Now, now, gentleman," he chided, "there's no need to say anything we're going to regret later. I can hear the Kaiser laughing right now when he finds out that our government is tearing itself to pieces over Martinique."

General Wood and President Lowden had been rivals for the Republican nomination in 1920, and it was clear that the Secretary of State still thought he would have made the better President. McCormick glanced sharply from one to the other. Lowden compressed his lips, biting back whatever he was about to say. Wood's face remained impassive, but his color, which had darkened, slowly faded.

"The President did not mean to imply that you have done anything but an exemplary job during this crisis," McCormick continued. "Isn't that right, sir?" he asked, staring at Lowden.

"Yes… yes, of course, Leonard," Lowden told his Secretary of State. "You still have my utmost confidence. I was simply taken by surprise by this new development, especially now, when we thought that the crisis was all but over. If I said anything that implied anything less than my complete satisfaction with your performance, please accept my apology."

"There is no need for any apologies, Mister President," Wood answered. "These last weeks have been a tremendous strain on all of us, particularly on you. It seems that whatever we do to relieve the situation, the tensions seem to grow rather than relax. I still believe that the Germans will not, *cannot* go to war with us under the current circumstances, but I will admit that my confidence in my ability to predict their behavior is less than it was. I do not believe that we should take the dispatch of the *Rheinland* to this hemisphere at face value. Do they truly think in Berlin that they can carve a path through the entire U.S. Navy with one old battleship? I cannot believe they are so foolish. In my opinion, this is simply another demonstration, another gesture, like the original announcement about accelerating the building schedule at the new base, and sending the two freighters. The Kaiser is raising the stakes, putting the question to us in a way that cannot be avoided."

"That question being: are we willing to risk a *casus belli* by firing on a German Imperial warship to enforce our blockade?" McCormick asked. "That is a question that only you can answer, Mr. President."

Lowden nodded. "True enough, Joseph. How much time do I have to think about it?"

"The *Rheinland* has a cruising speed of 12 knots," Wood said. "The Navy Department estimates that it will not arrive in the Caribbean before June 7."

"Two weeks," the President mused. "Thank you, General Wood. I will obviously need to bring this development before the full cabinet tomorrow. Please prepare a briefing on the subject for that meeting. I would like you to consult with the Navy Department, and include their estimates of the capabilities of the German battleship in your memorandum."

"Yes, sir. I will start on that right away," Wood said. He rose. "Good morning, Mr. President."

After the door closed behind the Secretary of State, Lowden swiveled his chair around to face his private secretary. "Well, Joseph, Kaiser Wilhelm is certainly not making this easy for us. What am I supposed to do now? What is the right decision?"

"I don't know if there is a 'right' decision, boss," McCormick answered. "I think what you have is a choice between bad and worse. But, let me ask you a question: how important is being re-elected to you?"

Lowden grimaced. "I suppose it would be easier if this was the last year of my second term, and I wasn't planning to run again. But you must believe me, Joseph, I have thought about it and I am ready to make the decision to go to war, even if it means losing the election next year, *if* I am convinced that it is absolutely necessary. But I'm *not* convinced, damn it."

"I believe you, boss," McCormick said. "If I had a crystal ball that showed the future, I could probably give you excellent advice based on what the history books twenty years from now will say about this crisis. They would know exactly what the right decision would have been. Unfortunately, we don't have the luxury of hindsight. This is one of those times when I remember how glad I am that I'm not sitting in your chair and I don't have to make these kinds of decisions. But I will tell you this: I don't know of another man in the country that I would rather have in your place right now. Boss, whatever you decide, I know it won't be based on consideration of what is best for your political career. I'm sure it will be what you believe is in the best interests of the United States."

"I appreciate your vote of confidence, Joseph," Lowden said. "Having your support makes the burden of this office much more bearable."

As was his habit when facing difficult decisions, Lowden remained alone in the Oval Office for a long time after his last appointment of day had concluded. As he stared out the windows of his office, watching the cloak of night settle over the streets of Washington, he wondered what his counterparts in Berlin were doing at that moment.

SMS Rheinland

CHAPTER FOURTEEN
OFF MARTINIQUE, JUNE 8, 1923

Vice-Admiral Hugh Rodman stood with his legs braced, well apart, and his hands together behind his back, the very image of calm confidence amid the air of growing tension on the bridge of the battleship *Nevada*. The veteran Rodman firmly believed that confidence in any naval unit began from the top command and spread all the way down to the ordinary seaman, as did its absence. He wanted every officer and man under his command in the Caribbean Battle Force to have the utmost confidence in competence of their comrades.

"There she is!" the young Lieutenant jg, who was peering through field glasses at a column of smoke on the horizon, cried excitedly. He must have realized that his announcement had been made in a voice that was a bit too loud and high-pitched, because he quickly added in much more measured tones, "Unidentified warship sighted, Admiral, ten degrees off the starboard bow. She appears to match the configuration of a *Nassau*-class battleship of the Imperial German Navy, sir. Warship is accompanied by two merchant vessels."

Rodman approved of the way the way the Lieutenant had regained control of his emotions, so he confined his response to a dry comment. "I think we can be reasonably confident that you have spotted S.M.S. *Rheinland*, Mr. Sprague. It would be most unsporting of the Germans to send any other ship, after they have gone to so much trouble to advertise the arrival of that one." The Admiral found it unnecessary to add that the German dreadnought and the two merchant ships it was escorting had already been identified by a destroyer of DesRon Three two hours earlier.

"Captain Luby, sound general quarters," Rodman ordered. As the controlled chaos of clamoring bells and officers shouting orders to men rushing to their battle stations erupted around him, he continued, speaking now to one of the men assigned to run messages to the radio room. "Signal to Task Force: Battle Group..." (this was the main battle line, consisting of six American dreadnought battleships: *Nevada*, where Rodman was flying his flag, *Oklahoma*, *Pennsylvania*, *Arizona*, *New Mexico* and *Tennessee*, all armed with 14-inch main batteries, and as far as Rodman was concerned, a match for any warships on the planet) "... execute Action Plan B, on course zero-seven-three, speed at 18 knots."

Rodman watched the maneuver through his field glasses, and was gratified by the smooth perfection with which his orders were executed, as the big ships gracefully formed a line to the stern of *Nevada*. It was evident that the weeks of rehearsing for this moment had not been in vain. Rodman was proud of his men and his ships, and he did not have the slightest doubt that they could sink anything the Germans sent against them. That fact the Germans dared to send out a single battleship, and an old one at that, to challenge the might of the U.S. Navy, was taken by the veteran Admiral as a personal insult. After he crossed the T of the little German column and put his battleships in position to annihilate the arrogant Prussians with broadsides of fourteen-inch armor-piercing shell, he wished he could then give the order to fire.

However, his orders from Washington made it absolutely clear that he did not have the authority to give such an order, unless the Germans *fired upon and actually scored a hit on an*

American ship. Unless these conditions were met, the Americans were not to offer violence to the Germans, even in self-defense.

On the other hand, they were permitted to put on as unfriendly a show of force as they could without actually shooting at the Germans. As they had ignored all his previous warnings to change their heading, which had been sent by radio, signal flag and blinker, Rodman decided that it was time to transmit one final message before playing his last and, he hoped, winning card.

"Take a new message to radio," Rodman told the runner. "'To S.M.S. *Rheinland*: the merchant ships you are escorting are entering a forbidden zone by order of the government of the United States. They are not permitted to continue to Martinique without inspection and approval by U.S. Naval personnel. You are ordered to reverse course immediately. I am authorized to take any steps necessary to enforce the interdiction. This is your final warning.' Send it immediately, son."

The runner scampered away, message in hand.

"What's your prediction, Luby?" Rodman asked the *Nevada*'s Captain as they waited for the German response. "What would you do if you were in command of that expedition?" He motioned with his chin in the direction of the *Rheinland* and her two charges.

"I don't know, Admiral," Luby said. "He'd have to be one cool customer to keep going. Even if he thinks we're bluffing, how could he possibly be sure enough to risk it? If the whole Battle Group opened up at once, that battleship would be blown clean out of the water, and the merchantmen…" He shook his head at the thought of what high caliber shellfire would do to the unprotected cargo vessels.

Rodman studied the big German battleship as they waited for an answer to the latest warning. *Rheinland*'s keel had been laid down in 1907, in a hasty response to the launching of the revolutionary *Dreadnought* one year earlier, and thus had some of the design peculiarities common to the earliest generation of the new super-battleships. Her main battery of twelve eleven-inch Krupp rifles disposed in six double turrets arranged in an unusual hexagonal configuration gave *Rheinland* the ability to fire as many as ten of the big guns forward or aft in salvo (although four of the ten would have very limited fields of fire), but only eight in broadside. This eccentric arrangement was not repeated in subsequent designs, and was unique to the *Nassau* class dreadnoughts of which *Rheinland* was a member. Rodman far preferred the centerline triple-gun turret design of *Nevada* and her sisters.

Although the *Nassau* class was built to meet the challenge laid down by Lord Fisher's *Dreadnought*, they were in a sense compromises, retaining some of the characteristics of older warships. In addition to the strange design of the main battery, the designers of *Nassau* had continued to use the older triple-expansion reciprocating engines, instead of switching to the marine turbines that powered all British capital ships built after 1906. Of course, the *Kaiserliche Marine* was not the only navy to shy away from the fuel-gulping turbine in its early dreadnoughts; two-shaft vertical triple-expansion engines also powered the first modern American types, the *South Carolina* class, which were laid down in 1906. The U.S. Navy did not build turbine-powered battleships until 1909, *Florida* and *Utah* being the first.

After fifteen minutes had passed, there was no reply to the radio message, indeed no response of any kind from the

Germans. This of course, was a reply of sorts, Rodman thought. Put into words, it was something like: *"Yeah? And if we don't, what are you going to do about it?"*

"Enemy column maintaining same course and speed, sir," reported Lieutenant Sprague.

"Captain Luby, I want 'A' turret..." (this was the forward turret) "...to fire a salvo of high explosive across the bow of that battleship at a range of 14,000 yards."

The order was echoed by the Captain, who repeated it to his gunnery officer, a Lieutenant Willis Lee. The gunnery officer immediately took readings from the range finder, a complex optical device mounted on a pivot on the bridge. Lieutenant Lee then repeated Rodman's order through a speaking tube to the plotting room below, along with the range and an exact time taken from his stopwatch. In a few seconds, the plotting room responded with the details of the target's course and speed. The gunnery officer now made some hurried calculations, and then picked up the tube again to pass his range and deflection readings on to the plotting room, which plotted them and passed the range and elevation figures to the guns.

Less than thirty seconds later, word came back from below that the guns were set at the proper range and elevation. Lieutenant Lee, still keeping the German ship centered in the range finder, pressed a button that produced a loud buzz. The buzz, which meant "stand by to fire" sounded at the same time inside "A" turret.

The gunnery officer waited, moved his thumb towards a large red button, hesitated, and then pressed the button, causing a deafening bell to ring in the turret. This was the signal to fire.

There was a tremendous blast, and three simultaneous

sheets of flame stabbed out to starboard from the Mark II 14-inch guns of *Nevada*'s forward turret. The recoil from the discharge caused *Nevada* to pitch suddenly to port, but the veteran bridge crew was prepared for this motion and not one of them lost his balance or even so much as acknowledged the sudden lurch.

Admiral Rodman, who had focused his field glasses on the approaching German dreadnought, grunted in satisfaction as three huge geysers leapt out of the sea three hundred yards ahead of the big German battleship.

"You have to know that miss was deliberate," he said, speaking to the German skipper. "Now turn your ships around before we get serious, Captain."

He watched in silence as the minutes went by and the Germans did not alter their speed by a single knot, or their course by so much as a degree.

"Shall we fire another salvo, Admiral Rodman?" Captain Luby asked.

Rodman lowered his binoculars, looked at the Captain and shook his head. "I don't really see the point," he said bleakly. "They obviously don't believe that we are going to actually fire on their ships. The Germans have called our bluff, Captain, and there is absolutely nothing we can do about it."

He grimaced. "Signal the Task Force to return to base," he told the radio room messenger. "I'll be in my quarters. Carry on."

Well, Rodman thought as he walked through the passageway, *we didn't start a war, today at least. But what happens next time?*

CHAPTER FIFTEEN
BERLIN, JUNE 10, 1923

The All-Highest, His Imperial Majesty Kaiser Wilhelm Hohenzollern, the Second of that name, Emperor of Germany and King of Prussia, was hard enough to abide when he was in a bad mood, Crown Prince Rupprecht thought. But when he was in a mood like this, exulting in victory and enthusiastically contrasting his clever boldness with his cabinet's dull-witted timidity, he was very nearly unbearable. Not for the first time since he had accepted Wilhelm's offer to join his cabinet as the Minister of War, Rupprecht considered the potential pleasures of an early retirement to his estates in Bavaria.

"Really, gentlemen, you should apply for positions in the American government," a jovial Wilhelm twitted the Crown Prince and Chancellor Michaelis. "I'm certain that you would get along splendidly with President Lowden, as you all three seem to think alike. You were just as much afraid of war as the Americans, and thus unable to see when opportunity beckoned, whereas *I* was capable of taking matters into my own hands and making history, instead of…"

He broke off as a messenger rushed into the room and delivered a folded sheet of paper to the Chancellor.

"My humble pardon for interrupting, Your Majesty," Michaelis said, "but this is from the Foreign Office, and is marked 'Urgent-Top Priority'." He opened the paper and scanned it quickly.

"I am afraid I have bad news, Your Majesty," he said,

raising his eyes to the Kaiser. "It seems that our celebration of victory in Martinique is a bit premature."

"What are you talking about?" Wilhelm snarled angrily. "The American curs have been whipped back into their kennel, and the day belongs to Germany."

By way of answer, Michaelis handed the paper to the Kaiser. As he read, his eyes began to bulge from his head.

"As you can see, Your Majesty," Michaelis said, "the Americans were not the only ones with an interest in our new naval base. The English..."

"My bastard English cousins are trying to snatch victory away from me!" Wilhelm shrieked, purpling. He crumpled the Foreign Office paper in his fist. "This is intolerable! They cannot get away with it!"

Prince Rupprecht retrieved the balled paper from where his sovereign had hurled it in his rage, and tried to smooth it out enough to make it legible.

"The British say that His Majesty's Government considers the base at La Trinity as touching on vital imperial interests, and they..." Michaelis began to explain.

"They say that they will send their Bermuda Squadron to Martinique to 'neutralize' La Trinitie unless we begin immediate negotiations with the Americans," the Crown Prince cut in, examining the British Note, and silently translating the diplomatese of the document into everyday German.

The Kaiser half-rose from his seat as he brought both fists thumping down on the table. "I will not tolerate this interference! We will send our own fleet; we will declare war and smash them! We will..." He broke off his tirade to glare at his two chief ministers, who were shaking their heads.

"*What*?!" Wilhelm demanded in exasperation.

"Your Majesty," Rupprecht said patiently, "if a naval war against the United States is hopeless, surely one against Great Britain promises even worse prospects. The British have by far the biggest and best navy in the world, as you well know, and..."

"...and a contemptible little army that my army could crush in a week, in a *day*," Wilhelm interrupted.

"If we could come to grips with it, Your Majesty," the Chancellor said. "Unless we were able to overcome the Royal Navy, any war with Great Britain would of necessity be a naval war. And, as Crown Prince Rupprecht points out, we cannot hope to win such a war. Indeed, we cannot even prevent the British from carrying out their threat to invade Martinique and 'neutralize' La Trinitie, whatever that may entail. We do not possess anything like the means to stop them from taking whatever actions they like in the Caribbean. And I do not think that the British are... what was the American term? 'Bluffing', yes. I do not believe that Mr. Churchill is the bluffing kind."

The Kaiser made no reply to Michaelis' observations, as their truth was so self-evident that he could think of nothing to say. He sat in silence for a long time, trembling with suppressed rage, his lips pulled back from his teeth, his gloved hands clenched in anger.

At length, an apparently happier thought occurred to him. Slowly, his hands relaxed and his features settled back to a more usual configuration.

"It occurs to me that I have still not dealt with the individuals who are responsible for placing me in such an embarrassing position," he said. "I have just now thought of an appropriate reward for my faithful servants, His Excellency, Gottlieb von Jagow and Grand Admiral Alfred von Tirpitz."

"The firing squad, Your Majesty?" Rupprecht asked interestedly. "It would be no less than they deserve."

"No, since they risked so much to further our overseas empire, it is only fair that they be permitted to continue to serve that empire in some fashion," the Kaiser said. His lips were curled in a smile, if one could call it that, one which would have sent small children running for their mothers, had any been there to see it. "I will make certain that they will be offered positions where they will be able to provide such service."

The Kaiser's "smile" vanished. "And if they reject that offer," Wilhelm said grimly, "*then* the firing squad."

CHAPTER SIXTEEN
From *The Philadelphia Inquirer*, June 18, 1923
By Raymond Swing, Foreign Affairs Editor

...The agreement between the two nations that brought the crisis over Martinique to a close was widely seen as a major diplomatic setback for Germany. The base, which had been intended to be the home for a new German Caribbean Fleet at La Trinitie, was sold to the United States Government for $1 million. In a statement released by the State Department, it was revealed that the government has already reached an agreement with a consortium of American and British steamship lines to develop the partially completed site as a new tourist destination and base for passenger liners in the Caribbean.

There has been no official explanation of the reason for the unexpectedly sudden resolution of the crisis, and both the American and German governments have refused to comment. It is widely speculated that the deadlock was broken by British intervention. Mr. Churchill's government has also declined to comment on this matter. However, the announcement today that Secretary of State Leonard Wood would travel to London next month for meetings with his counterpart Sir Edward Grey and Prime Minister Winston Churchill lends credence to this rumor.

Ultimately, the Martinique crisis may result in causing the United States and Great Britain to lay the foundation for an eventual agreement that will provide mutual security from future German attempts to expand in this part of the world.

In the view of this reporter, it is vital that the government of the United States and its citizens realize the potential threat posed by the German Empire, and begin to form relationships with other powers to control German aggression. It is hoped that the recently resolved crisis will serve to awaken Americans to the reality that in this era the oceans may no longer constitute complete protection from the rest of the world, and may in fact now be highways for foreign powers who wish to extend their reach to this hemisphere. A mutual defensive treaty with Great Britain would be an essential first step in ensuring the future security of the United States, and such a treaty should be reached and approved by the Senate as soon as possible.

CHAPTER SEVENTEEN
SEPTEMBER 23, 1923,
WILHELMSHAVEN, MARTINIQUE

As he walked down the wharf along after debarking with the other 150-odd passengers from the newly arrived S.S. *Dolphin* out of Tampa, Raymond Spruance stooped to peek under the brim of his wife's enormous white straw hat, to see how she was faring in the island's combination of 95 percent humidity and 85 degree heat under a blazing, bright sun. She was an Indiana native, and he was certain that she was not accustomed to these tropical conditions.

As he suspected, Margaret was already sweating profusely, although they had left the shade of the ship behind only a few moments earlier. Before he could say anything, she snapped, "There is no need to look at me that way, Raymond, and no call to ask me if I am sorry I made you take me to Martinique for vacation. I am quite comfortable, thank you."

He straightened again until he was certain that Margaret's hat blocked her view of his features before he allowed a grin to spread across his face. "I was just going to point out the Martinique customs shed to you, and warn you that we'll probably be standing out here in the sun for a good long while, waiting for them to pass this crowd through. The last time I was here…"

"I remember your story about the two customs men very well, Raymond," Margaret replied, stiffly "and I am quite prepared to stand in line for as long as necessary."

As they grew nearer to the shed, Spruance saw that the customs officials he had encountered during his visit in April were gone, replaced by two new men. In this case, the change was most definitely an improvement.

Neither one of the two customs agents gave the luggage anything more than the most casual glance. Indeed, they scarcely even took the time to look up at the tourists to confirm that the photographs in their passports matched the faces of the persons standing before them, so rapidly did the two men ply the rubber stamps that imprinted the visas.

"Actually, they seem to be moving quite rapidly," Margaret remarked, as the line advanced.

Spruance did not reply. He was studying the two sweating customs officials closely. One of them was a short man, with a small, neatly trimmed mustache and a thinning hairline. He looked out of place in his dark blue customs uniform. Spruance got the impression that the man would have been more at home in an expensively tailored suit. He also looked vaguely familiar, as if Spruance had seen his picture in the newspaper, although that seemed unlikely.

As he got close to the counter, Spruance saw that the second official was a huge man, whose bald head was balanced by an impressive display of snow-white whiskers. In the climate of Martinique, the long beard must have been a torment to him. What was particularly notable was the unusual shape of the beard: it forked just below his chin, and the ends were neatly trimmed in points, like inverted horns. The normally unflappable Spruance goggled at the man, rooted in place.

The bearded agent stamped Spruance's passport without looking up at the American. When he noticed that Spruance was still standing in front of him, he did look up, then motioned impatiently for him to move along with his hand, while grunting, "*Weitergehen!*"

"Come along dear," Margaret said, tugging at her husband's sleeve. "The porter is taking our luggage to the taxi stand."

Spruance obediently allowed his wife to lead him away, but he kept glancing back unbelievingly over his shoulder at the bearded customs official.

"Do you have any idea who that is back there, Margaret, that German customs agent?" he asked.

"No, dear, who is he? An old friend of yours from school?" she said, making a wild guess.

"No, no, of course not," he answered irritably. "That's Admiral..." he hesitated, then finished, "...that is, he looks exactly like... but no, that's impossible. It couldn't be him."

Back at the customs shed, the two men had completed the task of passing the American tourists through into Martinique, and were now securing the shed for the day, locking away the pens, customs forms, ink pads and rubber stamps.

"Hurry it up, Jagow," urged the former Naval Minister to Kaiser Wilhelm II, Grand Admiral Alfred von Tirpitz, "the heat is killing me." Then he added, as he did every day, "I wonder if I should have chosen the firing squad?"

(Wilhelmshaven) Fort de France, Martinique

AFTERWORD

Gray Tide in the East came in for criticism from a number of readers who insisted that Woodrow Wilson, who had arbitrated the peace treaty between Germany and France in that alternate history, would never have allowed Germany to acquire Martinique, as this would have been a clear violation of the Monroe Doctrine. This view is based on a misunderstanding of the meaning of the Monroe Doctrine, and is discussed in Chapter Three.

Monroe first set forth the doctrine that would later bear his name in his State of the Union address of 1823. In the pertinent part, he said:

> ...the American continents, by the free and independent condition which they have assumed and maintain, are henceforth not to be considered as subjects for future colonization by any European powers... We owe it, therefore, to candor and to the amicable relations existing between the United States and those powers to declare that we should consider any attempt on their part to extend their system to any portion of this hemisphere as dangerous to our peace and safety. *With the existing colonies or dependencies of any European power we have not interfered and shall not interfere* (italics added). But with the Governments who have declared their independence and maintained it, and whose independence we have, on great consideration and on just principles, acknowledged, we could not view any interposition for the purpose of oppressing them, or controlling in any other manner their destiny, by any European power in any other light than as the manifestation of an unfriendly disposition toward the United States

(*The Monroe Doctrine (1823). Basic Readings in U.S. Democracy. United States Department of State. Archived from the original on January 8, 2012*).

From the above text, it is clear that Monroe intended his policy to apply to the nations of the Western Hemisphere that had already won their independence, but not to colonies being transferred from one European Power to another, as in the case of Martinique in the story. Of course, the fact that the Monroe Doctrine did not apply to the Martinique situation did not mean that the building of a new naval base and the stationing of a powerful German squadron in the town of La Trinitie would not have constituted a profound threat to the security of the United States; it merely made President Lowden's position more difficult, as he was not easily able to justify intervention in the Caribbean on the basis of the Monroe Doctrine.

The Monroe Doctrine also plays a part in the conclusion of the story, when Great Britain snatches victory away from the Kaiser. The Monroe Doctrine was originated jointly by the United States and Great Britain, both of whom saw European intervention in the Western Hemisphere as a danger to their very different interests. Indeed, in the early years, enforcement of the Doctrine was entirely in the hands of the Royal Navy, as the young American Republic lacked the naval power that was a necessity for the task. British interest in enforcement of the Monroe Doctrine was primarily motivated by free trade principles, and this continued to be true at least until World War II, when the United States stepped into the world power role formerly held by Great Britain. For a detailed analysis of the origins of the Monroe Doctrine, see "The Relation of British Policy to the Declaration of the Monroe Doctrine" by

Leonard Axel Lawson, in *Studies in History Economics and Public Law, vol. 103*, (New York, 1922).

The political situation in the United States at the opening of this book has Progressive Republican Frank Lowden in the White House after the election of 1920, instead of Warren G. Harding. It is a fact that the First World War brought the Progressive Era of politics to an untimely end, something that probably would not have occurred in the world of *Gray Tide*.

One of the most important, if indirect consequences of the First World War was the collapse of the Romanov Dynasty in Russia, and its replacement with the Bolsheviks, the world's first Communist government. This only happened with the connivance of the Germans, who sent Lenin into Russia in 1917 with the hope that he would disrupt the government and help to knock Russia out of the war. He succeeded all too well.

But in *Gray Tide in the East*, this never happens. Germany wins the war against Russia quickly, and has no need to sponsor any wild-eyed revolutionaries. Thus, the Bolshevik revolution never takes place.

This is significant for American political history. Before America's entry into the war, the dominant political strain in the two major parties was towards increasing government regulation of big business, and the protection of the ordinary citizen from the depredations of the wealthy and powerful. The Progressive policies included: a National Health service, universal social insurance, an eight-hour workday, workman's compensation insurance, strict limits on and disclosure of campaign contributions, among many others (list taken from the Progressive Party platform of 1912). This was largely due to the increasing popularity of the Socialist Party, which tallied nearly 1 million votes in the election of 1912 and thereby frightened the established parties badly enough to make them adopt many of the Socialist policies.

However, the Bolshevik Revolution of 1917, the subsequent attempts at Communist revolutions in Europe and the supposedly Bolshevik-inspired wave of labor violence in America after the war, brought about a reaction to Socialism which culminated in the Great Red Scare of 1919-1920. A. Mitchell Palmer, Woodrow Wilson's Attorney General took advantage of this climate of fear to illegally arrest thousands of people for no better reason, in many cases, than their membership in left-wing political parties. In this poisonous atmosphere, the Socialist Party and the policies it supported came to be associated with the acts of bomb-throwing Anarchists and Bolsheviks (most of whom, it must be said, existed only in the imagination of A. Mitchell Palmer) in the eyes of many average Americans, and the policies it promoted, discredited. In this way, the First World War could be said to have indirectly rung the curtain down on the Progressive era before its time.

The pacifist political atmosphere in the United States of 1923 as portrayed here is reasonable in view of American attitudes towards the historical First World War prior to the sinking of the *Lusitania* in May, 1915. Even as late as the Fall of 1916, Americans overwhelming favored neutrality, as is shown by the success of Wilson's campaign with its slogan "He kept us out of war!"

In *Gray Tide in the East*, the G.E.W. (Great European War, a more appropriate name for the conflict described in that book than is World War One), ends in 1915, there is no submarine warfare, and no *Lusitania* sunk with 1198 civilians drowned, including 123 Americans. It is not unnatural to assume that, under these circumstances, America would have continued to live in a pacifist slumber, its people profoundly uninterested in anything that happened beyond the borders of their own country. Those readers who believe they detect a parallel between the Martinique Crisis depicted in this story and the Cuban Missile Crisis of 1962 are not mistaken. The diplomatic/military confrontation in the story is a version of the Kennedy-Khrushchev showdown transferred to an era of isolationism.

The famous cable from William Randolph Hearst to Frederick Remington, "You provide the pictures, I'll provide the war" (quoted by the Secretary of State in Chapter 5), turns out, upon inspection, to be a fabrication. It was apparently the invention of a Canadian journalist named James Creelman, and originated in his 1901 book *On the Great Highway: The Wanderings and Adventures of a Special Correspondent*. This bogus quote (in a slightly altered form) achieved immortality in the film *Citizen Kane*, and has now become inextricably linked with Hearst as an exemplar of his "yellow journalism", in spite of the fact that he almost certainly never said it. See *Yellow Journalism: Puncturing the Myths, Defining the Legacies* by Joseph W. Campbell, (Westport, Ct., 2012). See also:
http://www.ucpress.edu/content/chapters/11067.ch01.pdf

(For readers who wonder why I allowed General Wood to use the fake Hearst quote in the story, I thought it unlikely that he would be aware that the famous quote was a fabrication.)

For the details on the firing procedure on battleship *Nevada*, I relied upon a chapter on Fire Control from *Elementary Naval Ordnance and Gunnery*, by Lieutenant H. C. Ramsey USN (Boston, 1918), which was kindly extracted from the book and made available on the Internet by Byron Angel:
http://www.gwpda.org/naval/usnfirec.htm

For details on warships, *The Dreadnought Project*

(http://www.dreadnoughtproject.org) on which I relied heavily in the original *Gray Tide in the East*, once again proved invaluable.

Following are capsule biographies of the main historical characters who appear in the story, in order of appearance:

William Sowden Sims - Image from The Life of Admiral Hahan, Charles Carlisle
Taylor, 1920, London

William Sims (1858-1936), was a Rear Admiral at the time of
the United States' entry into the First World War. He was
placed in command of all U.S. naval forces in Europe, and
promoted to Vice Admiral by the war's end. He served two
tours as President of the Naval War College, and won a
Pulitzer Prize for his history of the U.S. Navy during World
War I.

Leiutenant Commander Raymond Spruance

Raymond Spruance (1886-1969), became one of the great fighting Admirals of the Second World War, and one of the greatest in American history. He commanded U.S. aircraft carriers at the Battle of Midway in 1942, the Battle of the Philippine Sea in 1944 and numerous other engagements, winning a reputation for intelligence and calm in even in moments of crisis, along with the nickname "electric brain". He was awarded the Navy Cross and the Distinguished Service Medal three times. For details of the early career of Raymond Spruance, see *The Quiet Warrior* by Thomas B. Buell, (Annapolis, 1987).

Sumner Welles by Underwood & Underwood –
the United States Library of Congress's Prints and Photographs division

Sumner Welles (1892-1962) was an American government official and career diplomat in the Foreign Service. He was a major foreign policy adviser to President Franklin D. Roosevelt and served as Secretary of State from 1937 to 1943. He is credited with being the man most responsible for the design of the United Nations.

Frank Orren Lowden – source unknown

Frank Lowden (1861-1943) is virtually forgotten today, but in 1920, along with Leonard Wood, he was the leading Republican candidate for President. Lowden was the Governor of Illinois and a Progressive. Coming into the Republican Convention that year, Lowden boasted more delegates than any other candidate: 211, to be precise. By the sixth ballot, his delegate total had risen to 311.5 of the 501 needed to win the nomination. On the same ballot, General Wood received an identical total of 311.5. (Evidently, one delegate could not decide between the two.) Had the two men reached the kind of agreement suggested in the story, Lowden would have taken the nomination on the next ballot. But they did not, and an exhausted convention finally chose the dark horse Warren G. Harding on the tenth ballot.

Joseph Medill McCormick 1912 by Moffett, Chicago
- the US Library of Congress Prints and Photographs Division

Joseph M. McCormick (1877-1925) Lowden's personal secretary in the book (he would have been called the White House Chief of Staff, had that job title existed in 1920) was in history a Representative and later junior Senator from Illinois. He was the older brother of "Colonel" Robert McCormick, publisher of the *Chicago Tribune*, who was famously opposed to American entry into World War II, and one of the leading opponents of the second Roosevelt in the press.

General Leonard Wood Rol BNF Gallica
by Agence Rol - Bibliothèque nationale de France.

Leonard Wood (1860-1927) was a physician who joined the U.S. Army in 1885, and eventually rose the rank of Lieutenant General and the position of Army Chief of Staff, the only medical officer ever to do so. He was the personal physician of two Presidents (Cleveland and McKinley), and the personal friend and political heir of a third, Theodore Roosevelt. Wood entered politics in 1920 at the urging of the former President's family after Roosevelt's death, running for the Republican nomination for President.

Gottlieb von Jagow circa 1915 by Bain - Library of Congress.

Gottlieb von Jagow (1863-1935) was a career diplomat who served as the German Foreign Minister from 1913-1916. He is thought to be the principal author of a German plan to ally Mexico with Japan and involve them in a war with the United States, in order to keep the U.S. out of the European war. This plan, made public through an intercepted telegram (the notorious Zimmerman Telegram), was the immediate cause of the U.S. entry into World War I in 1917.

Alfred von Tirpitz – the German Federal Archive (Deutsches Bundesarchiv)

Alfred von Tirpitz (1849-1930) was the principal architect of the Imperial German Navy, raising Germany from the status of a minor naval power in the 1890s to the one of the great naval powers in the world by 1912. He attained the highest rank available in the Imperial Navy, Grand Admiral, and was the Naval Minister from 1898 to 1916.

Rupprecht von Bayern by Bain News Service,
the United States Library of Congress's Prints and Photographs division.

Rupprecht Maria Luitpold Ferdinand, Crown Prince of Bavaria (1869-1955) was a professional soldier, as well as the heir to the Bavarian crown. He attained the rank of Lieutenant General by 1912, and commanded the Sixth Army in 1914. He was promoted to the rank of Field Marshal in 1916, in recognition of his military talents. He was one of the earliest advocates for peace in the German military hierarchy, deciding by the end of 1917 that the war was unwinnable after the American entry on the Allied side. He was disliked by Hitler, a feeling he reciprocated, and was forced into exile in 1939 to escape arrest. His wife, Princess Antoinette of Luxembourg, and his children were arrested in 1944, but they survived captivity in the Sachsenhausen and Dachau concentration camps until they were liberated in 1945.

Kaiser Wilhelm II from the collections of the Imperial War Museums.

Kaiser Wilhelm II (1859-1941) was the last Emperor of Germany, ruling from 1888 to 1918. His intelligence was offset by an erratic temperament that led him to make impulsive decisions, especially in the area of foreign policy. Although he was not truly a warmonger, he gained that reputation through his careless actions and intemperate language, which gave rise to several international crises. He was obsessed with assuring Germany's "place in the sun," and had a life-long fixed belief that Great Britain was plotting to keep him and the his Empire in the shade. He was forced to abdicate in 1918, when it became apparent that the war was lost.

Georg Michaelis - the German Federal Archive (Deutsches Bundesarchiv)

Georg Michaelis (1857-1936), served as Chancellor of Germany and Minister President of Prussia for a short time in 1917, following the dismissal of his predecessor, Theobold von Bethmann-Hollweg. He has the distinction of being the only commoner to serve as the chief minister in the 400 year history of the Hohenzollern dynasty.

Edward Grey 1914 by Bassano – W Harris & Ewing Collection, Library of Congress.

Sir Edward Grey (1862-1933) was a Liberal politician and the Foreign Secretary of Great Britain from 1905 to 1916, the longest continuous tenure of any man in that office. From the time he took office, Grey's goal was to support the balance of power in Europe by committing the British Empire to an alliance with France and Russia (the so-called *entente cordiale*), and thus restrain the Central Powers, led by Germany. He was unable to bring Great Britain into a military alliance with these powers by 1914, and it was the German invasion of Belgium that constituted the *casus belli* for Britain's entry into World War I. He left office in 1916, when the Asquith government fell from power, and served for a short time as the ambassador to the United States. He was elevated to a peerage in 1916, as Viscount Grey of Fallodon.

Admiral Scheer by Bain News Service -
the United States Library of Congress's Prints and Photographs division

Reinhard Scheer (1863-1928) was a German Admiral who commanded the High Seas Fleet (the main battle fleet) at the Battle of Jutland in 1916. He was subsequently promoted to Chief of Naval Staff, in which post he served until the end of the war. He received numerous military honors for his service in the Imperial Navy, including the Iron Cross, 1st and 2nd Class, Pour le Merit, and the Knight's Cross of the Royal Order of Hohenzollern, among many others.

Claude Bloch (1878-1967) served in the United States Navy from 1899 to 1945, retiring with the rank of Full Admiral. He was the Commander-in Chief of the Navy from 1938 to 1940. He was awarded the Navy Cross for his service as the commander of the transport *U.S.S. Plattsburg* during World War I. Bloch was the highest ranking Jewish officer in the armed forces until well after the end of the Second World War.

William Leahy by United States Navy

William Leahy (1875-1959), rose to the rank of Fleet Admiral during a naval career that spanned more than four decades. He held the post of Chief of Naval Operations from 1937 to 1939, when he retired from active duty, for the first time. He served as Governor of Puerto Rico and Ambassador to France before the United States entered World War II. In 1942 he was appointed to the new position of Chief of Staff to the Commander in Chief, which later would be renamed Chairman of the Joint Chiefs of Staff. He advised Truman against the use of the atomic bomb on Japan on moral grounds, but this advice was disregarded. He was awarded the Navy Cross and the Navy Distinguished Service Medal in the course of his long career.

Hugh Rodman circa 1915 - the United States Library of Congress's Prints and Photographs division.

Hugh Rodman (1859-1940) served in the U.S. Navy from 1880 to 1923, reaching the rank of Admiral. He saw his first action at the Battle of Manila Bay in 1898 during the Spanish-American War. In 1917, as a Rear Admiral, he was placed in command of Battleship Division Nine, which consisted of four (later increased to five) battleships and sent to fight in Europe. Once there, his command operated under Admiral David Beatty as the Sixth Battle Squadron of the Grand Fleet (Royal Navy) in the North Sea until the end of the war. For this service, he was made a Knight of the Order of Bath by King George V. He was the Commander-in-Chief of the Pacific Fleet from 1919 to 1921, and later represented the United States at the coronation of King George VI in 1937.

Winston Churchill circa 1921 – National Library of Ireland

Winston Churchill (1874-1965) was twice the Prime Minister of Great Britain during a political career that began in with his election to the House of Commons in 1900 and lasted until his retirement in 1964. In between, at one time or another held practically every cabinet position including First Lord of the Admiralty (twice), President of the Board of Trade, Chancellor of the Exchequer and many others. His reputation was damaged by the failure of the Gallipoli Campaign in World War I for which he was blamed, and which was probably was the reason that he did not become Prime Minister until 1940. Besides being a politician, he was a writer and Nobel Prize Laureate, artist, war correspondent and army officer.

Raymond Gram Swing by Chicago Daily News – The Library of Congress

Raymond Gram Swing (1887-1968) was a journalist and head of the *Chicago Daily News* Berlin bureau in 1914. He was a war correspondent who covered the 1915 Gallipoli campaign from the Turkish side among many other battles of the First World War. He later became a pioneer in radio journalism. His radio coverage of the 1932 presidential election brought him an offer from CBS to set up a radio news network in Europe. He turned down this offer, and the position was given to Edward R. Murrow. He later signed in 1936 with the Mutual Radio Network, covering Europe, and went on to a long and distinguished career in broadcasting with ABC, BBC and the Voice of America.

Book Two
Rip-Tide

Rip-tide: a strong, dangerous undercurrent, running from the shoreline out to sea, usually caused by powerful off-shore winds. A rip-tide is often the first warning sign of an approaching storm.

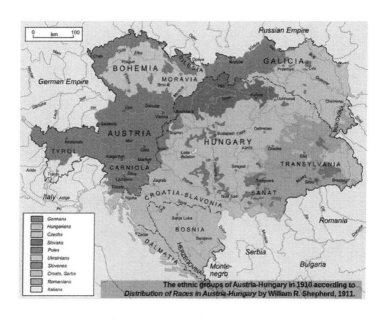

The ethnic groups of Austria-Hungary in 1910 according to
Distribution of Races in Austria-Hungary by William R. Shepherd, 1911.

CHAPTER ONE
VIENNA, JULY 16, 1923

Prince Sixtus Ferdinand Maria Ignazio Alfred Robert Bourbon, Duke of Parma, bent over a massive mahogany Biedermeier billiards table, peering down the shaft of his cue stick as he calculated a tricky carom shot. His left eye was shut, and he was squinting with the right through the cloud of aromatic smoke produced by the Maria Guerrero Cuban cigar which was clenched in his teeth. He was in the billiards room on the second floor of the *Schloss* Schönbrunn Palace, the summer home of the Hapsburgs.

"It is an easier game when you can actually see the ball you are aiming for, Sixtus," commented the man seated on the long velvet-embroidered bench beneath an enormous oil painting of the investiture of the Order of Maria Theresa in 1758. He was an ordinary-looking man in his mid-thirties, and it was not his fault that he was His Imperial and Royal Apostolic Majesty, Charles the First, by Grace of God Emperor of the Austrian Empire, Apostolic Fourth King of that name of the Kingdom of Hungary, King of Bohemia and the Kingdom of Dalmatia, Croatia, Slavonia and the Kingdom of Galicia and Lodomeria, the Kingdom of Illyria, King of the Kingdom of Jerusalem, Archduke of Austria, Grand Duke of Tuscany and the Grand Duchy of Cracow, Duke of Lorraine and of the Archbishopric of Salzburg, of the Duchy of Styria, of the Duchy of Carinthia, of the Duchy of Carniola and of Bukovina, Grand Prince of Transylvania, Margrave of the

March of Moravia, Duke of Upper Silesia and Lower Silesia, of the Duchy of Modena, the Duchy of Parma, Piacenza, Guastalla… and so on and so forth.

Whenever possible, he preferred to be addressed as "Karl".

"Am I to suppose that you are handicapping yourself with that cigar to ensure that you do not commit an act of *lèse-majesté* by defeating your sovereign at billiards?" the Emperor asked.

The Prince made a quick motion of the arm, which held the butt-end of the cue-stick, and there was a *clack*! as the white ball collided with its target. He grunted in disappointment, and straightened as the seven-ball struck a cushion an inch to the left of the corner pocket and spun away across the expanse of green felt.

"Hah! He speaks at last," Sixtus said, turning to face the Emperor. "Those are your first words since dinner. I was beginning to think that whatever was troubling your Royal and Imperial mind would render you mute all evening."

Karl stroked his mustache. "I must beg your pardon for being such poor company this evening, Sixtus," he said. "I was given bad news just before we sat down to our meal, and I fear that I have been preoccupied with it all evening, to the point of rudeness."

"Karl, you know that you can tell me the news, whatever it is," Sixtus said. He laid the pool cue on the green felt tabletop, and walked over to sit down on the bench next to the Emperor. "As your Prime Minister, it is my duty to advise you on matters of state; and as your brother-in-law and friend I am always ready to share the burden of governance with you, when the weight of the crown grows too heavy."

"I was just about to tell you about it, Sixtus," Karl said. He reached inside his jacket and removed an envelope, which he handed to his companion. "Here," he said, "you can read it for yourself."

The Prince dubiously eyed the embossed coat of arms on the envelope: a black eagle with a red beak and talons, wearing a shield depicting another eagle, this one black and gold, the whole surmounted by a jewel-encrusted crown, the all-too-familiar coat of arms of the German Empire. "A little note from our dear imperial cousin Wilhelm, I suppose?" he asked.

The Emperor nodded.

"Now what can be on his alleged mind?" Sixtus asked as he opened the envelope and fished out the letter inside. He read rapidly, and then looked up at Karl, his face beginning to flush with anger.

"Now he has the arrogance to tell us how to handle ethnic minorities in our own Empire?" he demanded indignantly. He began to read aloud from the letter. " 'I have recently become aware of unrest in the Ukrainian territories added to Austria in 1915. Certain nationalist demagogues have dared to denounce your Imperial Majesty at mass public rallies in Kiev and other cities, even going so far as to incite these mobs to revolutionary activity...'" (Austria-Hungary had acquired most of the southern half of the Ukraine from Russia under the Treaty of Cracow that ended the war in the east in 1915) "...The success of these demonstrations has also emboldened other rabble-rousers in Ruthenia, Slovakia and Bohemia to commit similar outrages. There is only one way to handle these troublemakers: the ring-leaders should be immediately arrested, and then lined up in front of a wall and shot! As your fellow-Emperor and one with somewhat more experience in these matters, I strongly advise you to take stern and immediate action. If this unrest is not quelled without delay, it may even spread to my realm, where, I can assure you, it will not be permitted. If you find that you are not in a position to squelch these revolutionaries by using the stern measures that the times require, dear Charles, I will be more than glad to provide a few divisions of my Prussian Guards to aid you in putting a decisive end to the problem...'."

The Prince trailed off, staring down at the letter in his hand again, as if not quite believing what he had just read, then looked up at his brother-in-law. "As is usual with Wilhelm, his threats have all the subtlety of a highway robber pointing a pistol at your head," he said at length. "If we do not put down the anti-government protests in the Ukraine in the Prussian style, at the point of a bayonet, he will provide 'aid' in the form of his spike-helmeted legions to do it for us. And he is even willing to extend the offer to Ruthenia, Slovakia and Bohemia. How generous of him!" he said ironically. "The Kaiser's concern is touching, although a bit puzzling, I must admit. I am trying to recall exactly when Bohemia was part of Germany, but I confess I am failing. As I remember it, Bohemia has been part of the Empire since the Thirty Years War, a matter of some three hundred years or so."

"For my part," said the Emperor, "I wonder how quickly those Prussian Guards would leave our territory once they were established here. I also wonder what the Hungarian reaction would be to German encouragement of their favored methods of controlling their own ethnic minorities."

Here, Karl was bringing up a long-standing quarrel between the two halves of the Dual Monarchy. The system that had been established by the Compromise of 1867 included the creation of separate governments in Vienna and Budapest, with two independent parliaments linked only by the person of the Emperor-King. In the Austrian portion, known as Cisleithania, Karl's policy had been to deal with ethic unrest by granting rights to various minorities such as the Czechs, Poles, Slovaks, Slovenes, Croats, Serbs and others, so that they would be content to remain in the Empire, instead of seeking to form independent states. To further this policy, the Emperor had forced the Austrian parliament to adopt a Plan of Federation two years earlier, a multiethnic and democratic federation based on the consensus of nations. This plan was gradually transforming the western half of the Empire, taking political power from the Germans, who had formerly controlled Austria, and sharing it with the various ethnic minorities.

Thus far, however, Karl had been unable to overcome the resistance of the ruling Hungarians in the other half of the Dual Monarchy. The Hungarians, who were in complete control of the levers of power in the Transleithania, had absolutely no use for such radical ideas as Federalism. Instead, the government in Budapest preferred to apply a policy of Magyarization to its ethnic minorities (which included Slovenes, Romanians, Italians, Ruthenians, Serbs, among others). Under this program, all ethnic groups were to be assimilated into an indivisible Hungarian nation, by force if necessary. All state and private business was to be conducted in Hungarian, and Hungarian was the only language permitted in the state schools, this despite the fact that less than half of the population of Transleithania was Hungarian. The government in Budapest dealt roughly with ethnic and nationalist protestors, not hesitating to arrest ethnic agitators and hold them indefinitely, and would no doubt have been happy to apply the even more forceful methods suggested by the Kaiser, if not for the restraints imposed on them by the King.

"So, this impertinent letter has provided the impetus for you to follow my advice at last?" the Prince asked. "I thought it was more than enough provocation when Wilhelm forced that Tariff and Trade Agreement down our throats. How strange that steel, heavy machinery, chemicals and textiles, all *German* net exports ended up on the tariff-free list, while somehow coal, petroleum, raw timber and agricultural products, *our* exports, were still subject to import duties in the German Empire. If that was not enough, he then contrived to nearly drag us into a war with the English and the Americans over some tiny island no one has ever heard of in the Caribbean Sea, and now…"

"I am aware of the recent history of relations between ourselves and Germany. Indeed, I am all too aware of it," Karl interrupted. "I must remind you that I never opposed your advice, Sixtus. I agree that it is absolutely essential we find a way out of the embrace of Germany before the Empire becomes nothing more than another German dependency. It was never a question of if, but only one of when and how. The when is decided. This evening, as I sat here, I came to the conclusion that we must act now to pull ourselves out of the German orbit. If we put off action any longer, I fear we will lose the ability to act at all. In fact, this was the very matter weighing so heavily on my mind this evening. Now there is only one question remaining: how do we go about it without alerting Berlin in advance?"

"Certainly, it would never do to allow Wilhelm to know what we are doing, at least until we can at least arrange a high-level meeting with our new potential allies," Sixtus said. "We cannot use the normal diplomatic channels, that much is certain. The Foreign Ministry is rotten with German agents, and they probably have a spies in every one of our embassies."

"Exactly," the Emperor agreed. "It was this which troubled me rather more than whether the attempt should be made at all."

Prince Sixtus smiled. "Fortunately for you, my dear brother-in-law, your realm is blessed with not only an excellent Prime Minister, but also an efficient and intelligent Minister of the Interior," he said. "What is more, these two extraordinary civil servants occupy a single body, which is present, and at your service." He rose and made a sweeping bow.

"Yes, yes, " Karl said, waving him back down again. "I am aware that you are a veritable one-man cabinet, Sixtus, but I do not see how that provides the answer to our problems."

The Prince resumed his seat. "It's quite simple, really. I anticipated that the day when you would reach the decision to break from Germany would come soon, and I therefore made appropriate plans for that day. As you may recall, as part of the reorganization of the government, I had the military intelligence agency placed under the Interior Ministry, to maintain civilian oversight, after the Redl scandal had damaged it so badly." Colonel Alfred Redl had been the head of the Austrian espionage service for many years, until he blew his brains out when it was discovered that he was actually in the pay of the Russians. "Since I knew that we could not entrust the matter to our own diplomats, I ordered an investigation to find the right man for the undertaking." He paused.

"And so?" Karl prompted.

"The man we wanted cannot be a diplomat, since anyone we selected would almost certainly be the immediate object of German scrutiny," the Prince replied. "Our man, whoever he is, would have to be able to meet with heads of various governments without drawing suspicion. He would also have to be both discreet and trustworthy, and we would certainly require someone who is sympathetic to our cause. For our purposes, we could do no better than an American journalist named Raymond Swing."

"A newspaper reporter?" Karl asked doubtfully. "Are you quite certain that we want to entrust state secrets of this magnitude to a reporter, Sixtus? I should think that the temptation to make a great splash by writing up the story for his newspaper would be overwhelming to such a man."

"Not this man," Sixtus said, shaking his head. "He can be trusted. He has already been used as a diplomatic courier, back in 1914, and his discretion is well established. Also, we will make it well worth his while carry out our mission. In addition to that, Swing has been writing articles about the threat posed by Germany for years, so that he has every reason to want us to succeed. I have copies of some of his articles translated into German. He is constantly urging the United States to join a coalition of other Powers to control Germany. Read them, and see if you do not think he is not already our man."

Karl waved his hand in dismissal. "That will not be necessary. Your assurances are quite sufficient for me. I assume it is unnecessary for me to worry about exactly how he will be contacted, or what will be the ostensible reason for him to come to Vienna. Certainly, a minister as accomplished and efficient as yourself would have already formulated a solution for such elementary difficulties." There was a mild touch of irony in his final words.

"Your Majesty is correct as usual," the Prince answered. "Everything has been arranged, and it remains only for me to give the word, and the machinery will be set in motion. Swing will be invited to the Schönbrunn Palace for an exclusive interview, which will be in the first of a series with leaders of the various European governments. We will arrange matters so that Swing will be invited to meet with M. Millerand..." the current French Prime Minister, "... Mr. Churchill, and

President Lowden, after his return to the United States, under circumstances where he will be able to deliver our message to them in private."

"I trust that he will also request interviews with Kaiser Wilhelm, Mr. Guchov and Signore Giolotti..." the last being the Prime Ministers of Italy and the Russian Union, respectively, "...to allay German suspicions," the Emperor said.

"Certainly they will all be asked, as will the heads of other nations as well," Sixtus assured him, "although I rather doubt that all of them will agree to meet with him. Given what he has already written about Germany, I deem it unlikely that Wilhelm, for one, will talk to him. Every eventuality has been examined and allowed for. Now, as long as nothing untoward happens, the plan is absolutely guaranteed to succeed..."

"Unless, of course, it does not," the Emperor finished for him.

"Precisely so, Your Majesty," Sixtus acknowledged. He rose and bowed again.

Shoenbrunn Palace, Vienna

The Billiards Room, Shoenbrunn Palace

The Walnut Room, Shoenbrunn Palace

CHAPTER TWO
PHILADELPHIA, JULY 19, 1923

It had been an irritating morning for the Managing Editor of the Philadelphia Inquirer. He had hardly been sitting at his desk long enough to review the big story on the poison ring, when a call from his bookie came in. Naturally, he had to drop everything and talk to the fellow. The man was completely unreasonable. The bookie had been threatening to ruin him by putting the word all over town that John Curtis did not pay off his gambling debts, unless he was paid in full, immediately. Curtis was having a harder and harder time putting him off. All this fuss over a trifling few thousand dollars!

But the call this morning was not a new demand for money. Instead, Curtis was told that his debt would be taken care of, so long as he agreed to meet a man with the unlikely name of **Ausstehend** in his office at 9 o'clock. What could he do but agree?

There was a sharp rap on his door. His secretary opened the door and stuck her head inside. "A Mr. Auster... hand?" Betty said uncertainly, stumbling over the unusual name, "...is here to see you, boss."

"Right," Curtis said resignedly. "Send him in, please."

His unwanted visitor was a tall man, who Curtis guessed was in his mid-thirties. He was dressed in what was obviously a tailored suit, and an expensive one at that. He looked both wealthy and European. From the name, he supposed that the man was either German or Austrian.

"Good morning, Mr. Curtis. May I sit?" Ausstehend's English instructor had evidently been British, judging by his accent, but Curtis was reasonably certain that his visitor was not a subject of King George V.

"Yes, of course, please take a seat," Curtis said, indicating a wooden chairs in front of his desk.

Ausstehend placed his Homburg on the desk and offered a kid-gloved hand for Curtis to shake. "A pleasure to meet you, Mr. Ausstehend." Curtis said, taking the hand. "You have a rather unusual name, if you don't mind my saying so."

The man displayed a tight smile. "Ausstehend is merely a convenience, not my actual name, naturally. It is the German word for 'unpaid'."

He sat and said, "I realize that you are a busy man, Mr. Curtis, so I do not propose to take any more of your time than absolutely necessary. I am here on behalf of my employers to ask a few simple favors of you. You will not suffer from cooperating with their requests; indeed, you will find that they are most generous."

Curtis wondered whether the man was some sort of criminal. If not, why would he use a pseudonym? "Perhaps you should get right to your business, Mr... whatever your name is, before I decide to throw you out of my office."

"Oh, I think that would be a mistake," the man said. He reached inside his jacket and retrieved a folded slip of paper. He dropped the paper on the desk. "Open it, Mr. Curtis. It is a token of my employer's good intentions."

Curtis unfolded the paper, glanced down at it, and then looked back up at his visitor. "This is my I.O.U. to Marrucci..." (this was Curtis' importunate bookie) "...and it's marked 'paid'. Now what do you want from me that would be worth that kind of money, I wonder?" he asked suspiciously.

"I will tell you right now, sir, you are wasting your time if you expect me to agree to involve myself or my newspaper in any illegal activity."

"No, no, Mr. Curtis, you need have absolutely nothing of the sort to fear," the man said. "I have only two requests, neither of which is illegal or immoral. On the contrary, I expect your newspaper to derive considerable benefit from our association."

Curtis' suspicions were allayed, at least temporarily. "All right then, what do you have in mind, exactly?" he asked.

"I want you to ask one of your employees, Mr. Raymond Swing, I believe he is your foreign affairs editor, to travel to Europe for the purpose of interviewing the leaders of Russia, Austria-Hungary, Germany, Italy, France and Great Britain, on the current state of international relations on the continent," the man said. "We will ask you to sign off on letters to the various governments requesting the interviews."

This was not even remotely like anything Curtis was expecting. He sat back in his chair, and contemplated the anonymous man in silence for a time. "Well," he said at last, "I agree that would be a nice series for the *Inquirer* to run. What I don't see is why you think the leaders of those countries will agree to interviews with an American reporter. I also can't help but wonder what's in it for you, or rather for your employer, whoever that may be."

"As to the second question, while your curiosity is perfectly understandable, I am not at liberty to offer an explanation at this time. I have no doubt that the reasons for the request will become clear in the future," the man said. "With regard to actually securing the interviews, I can promise you that at least some of the European leaders will consent to meet your man, if you allow us to arrange the inquiries. We only need your permission, and Mr. Swing, of course."

Curtis thought it over. He could not think of any way this proposal could hurt either him or the *Inquirer*. He nodded. "O.K. I agree. Swing's been talking about going back over to Europe anyway. If you can actually get him these interviews, he'll be happier than a pig in..." he paused and finished, "...clover." When he saw that this metaphor was received with a blank face by his visitor, he said, "I'm sure that Mr. Swing would be very interested to take the assignment."

"So, unless there's something else we need to discuss further," Curtis said, picking up the phone, "why don't I ask Ray Swing to come down here to meet you and hear your proposition?" He spoke a few quiet words into the phone, and then hung up.

"While we're waiting, why don't we pass the time playing a little game?" Curtis asked. "I'll try to guess who is employing you and why, and you'll try to keep a poker face when I name the right one. Doesn't that sound like fun?"

The man allowed himself a humorless smile. "It is my observation that people are able to derive amusement from any number of activities. Some take pleasure from playing cards, some chess, and some even find diversion wagering on horse races..." Curtis made a sour face to acknowledge this dig. "... so I do not doubt that you would find a pastime such as you have suggested to be diverting, Mr. Curtis. I, however, would not, and I trust you will not be offended if I decline to participate in your little game."

CHAPTER THREE
BERLIN, JULY 29, 1923

The cabinet meeting had just ended, and the big room was echoing with the sounds of a dozen hushed conversations between the Kaiser's ministers and their assistants as they exited the great hall.

Unlike his colleagues, the Foreign Minister, Franz von Papen did not walk out with his underlings. Instead, he waved them off and followed the Kaiser to the door that led to his private apartments in the Stadtschloss.

"Excuse me, Your Majesty," Papen said, "there was one other matter which I should bring to your attention."

Kaiser Wilhelm turned to look at his Foreign Minister. "Then why did you not mention it at the cabinet meeting, Papen?" he asked irritably. Wilhelm had plucked the Catholic Center party politician from obscurity because he was an aristocrat and, more importantly, because he was considered by both his friends and foes alike to be a man who had virtually no ideas of his own, and would therefore be easy to manage. The Kaiser wanted to keep foreign affairs in his own hands as much as possible, as he had a very high opinion of his own diplomatic abilities and a correspondingly low opinion of everyone else's. He did not much care for his Foreign Minister, finding him rather dull-witted, and as a Catholic, personally distasteful. "The purpose of these cabinet meetings is for my ministers to inform me about those matters of state which they wish to bring to my attention," Wilhelm caustically reminded Papen.

If Papen took the slightest offense at this insult to his intelligence, or even noticed the Kaiser's sarcasm, he gave no sign. "This was a matter which Your Majesty instructed me to bring to you privately, rather than at cabinet meetings."

Wilhelm scowled. "Oh, very well then, come along," he said ungraciously. "You can tell me about whatever it is while I am changing."

A tall soldier in the full uniform of the Imperial Guards, including a spiked helmet with the German eagle in silver across the brow and a gilded cuirass, opened the door for the Kaiser. Followed by Papen, he entered a small room furnished in Louis XIV. There was a marble-topped desk, a few upholstered chairs and a medium sized sofa, all carved with the elaborate curlicues characteristic of the period. There was also a tall standing cabinet decorated with paintings of Arcadian landscapes on the front panels. As the Kaiser entered, a servant flung open the doors of this cabinet to reveal a dozen outfits. At the same time, another servant rushed up to Wilhelm, and helped him to slip off the medal-encrusted Field Marshal's coat, which he had worn at the cabinet meeting.

"Don't bother to get comfortable, Papen," the Kaiser said, as his servants bustled around him, exchanging his military pants, blouse and coat for more comfortable and rugged hunting gear. "I have a weekend of hunting planned, and I am off to Rominten…" the royal hunting lodge on his East Prussian game preserve "…as soon as I have finished my business here. So say what you have to say, and be gone."

"Your Majesty, it concerns your Enemies of the Fatherland List," the Foreign Minister replied. This was a secret list of evil-minded foreigners who the Kaiser believed were actively trying to destroy Germany and/or himself (not that he differentiated between the two). Winston Churchill and Sir Edward Grey had prominent places on the list, as did a number of other influential politicians and writers. Wilhelm had assigned Papen's ministry the duty of keeping track of the doings of these dangerous foreigners. "It concerns the American reporter, Raymond Swing. He…"

"I remember him," Wilhelm interrupted. "The man is a viper. We extended every courtesy and convenience to him during the war, helped him in every way to perform his war reporting duties, and he has done nothing but display his ingratitude ever since, spewing out vicious, vile lies about Germany and myself."

"Just so, Your Majesty," Papen agreed. "It has been learned that he about to embark on a tour of the capitals of Continental powers, to interview their heads of government…"

"I do not recall receiving any such invitation!" Wilhelm exclaimed in outrage. "The man does not merely slander the good name of Germany, he now has the temerity to insult me personally!"

"Actually, Your Majesty, I believe that a request for an interview was sent to you by his newspaper," Papen said, correcting the Kaiser in an apologetic tone. "But knowing your feelings towards the man… well justified feelings!…" he hastened to add, "…it was thought best not to trouble you by bringing his insulting and ridiculous request to your attention."

"Yes, that is quite correct," Wilhelm said, mollified. "Indeed, I wonder that anyone would care to waste time answering questions from such an incompetent, untrustworthy hack. Who has agreed to meet him?"

"His itinerary thus far includes Brussels, Amsterdam, Vienna, Bucharest, Rome, London, and Paris," Papen said, "but more stops are expected to be added as more governments respond."

"Vienna?" the Kaiser asked. "Emperor Charles has agreed to give the swine an interview?"

"Evidently so, Your Majesty," Papen answered.

Wilhelm tugged at his mustache and frowned ferociously, indications that he was deep in the throes of thought. "This man Swing is nothing but a troublemaker, and I suspect that he is up to no good. I have a kind of special sense for these kinds of things, you know," he said. "I can't think why Charles would speak to him, unless..." The Kaiser paused. "The timing makes me wonder whether the Austrians have somehow gotten wind of our little operation in Budapest, and these interviews are somehow related to it. Have our people in the Austrian Foreign Ministry heard anything to indicate a breach in our security?" he demanded, frowning.

"Oh no, Sire," Papen assured him. "There is not the slightest reason to think that the Austrians know anything about it. Anything concerning the Budapest matter is assigned the highest priority; Your Majesty, would have been informed immediately if there was any such development, or even the suspicion of one."

Wilhelm nodded. "Even so, I do not trust the man, or the Austrians, for that matter, especially that Bourbon-Parma fellow. Have the American scribbler kept under observation, and report to me any suspicious activity our agents uncover. That is all, Papen. You are dismissed." With this, the Kaiser swept from the room, his Foreign Minister forgotten, his mind now completely occupied with the prospects for deer on his East Prussian estate.

Franz von Papen

The Throne Room at the Stadtschloss, Berlin
Photograph by Lukas Verlag

CHAPTER FOUR
BUDAPEST, AUGUST 14, 1923

Although it could boast neither the age and venerability of the Houses of Parliament in London nor the fame of the Capitol Building in Washington, the *Országház*, home of the Hungarian *Diet*, was nonetheless an impressive building, both inside and out. The walls of the chamber where the deputies met, which rose high overhead to a distant ceiling, were decorated in Slavonian oak carved in intricate detail, while at the front of the vast hall, the Speaker (which is to say, the Prime Minister of Hungary) sat surrounded by clerks and the other ministers of His Majesty's government behind a lectern that resembled nothing so much as an oversized pulpit. In fact, the chamber looked very much like a very large High Gothic cathedral crossed with a British courtroom. This was precisely the effect the architect had intended to make with his Gothic Revival design. It was in short, a very imposing building. In certain respects, it was sometimes almost too imposing, as on the not infrequent occasions when the sheer size of the legislative chamber combined with its indifferent acoustics would overwhelm even the most enthralling orator. On this particular morning, the Deputies were not being treated to anything like the most diverting speaker, nor the most inspiring subject.

It was a typical day in the Diet of Hungary. Fewer than half of the seats in the great hall were occupied, and those relatively few occupants were displaying obvious signs that they wished they were elsewhere, while the white-bearded Professor Tomas Masayrk, elderly leader of the Young Czech Party (Masaryk was 73 years old) droned on in support of a new proposal for reorganizing the Kingdom of Hungary. This proposal had just been sent to the Diet by His Apostolic Majesty, King Charles IV (who was known as Emperor Charles I when he was wearing his Austrian hat) for its consideration.

As the Professor's words echoed in the great, high-ceilinged chamber, they were greeted with indifference or hostility from his auditors. Even the Prime Minister, Count Tisza, generally the soul of politeness, could not summon the energy to make a show of interest in Masayrk's speech. It was all Tisza could manage to keep from dozing off. Even for this legislative body, which had never been accused of being especially alert, the air of boredom and inattentiveness was almost palpable.

Possibly this was due to the heat wave, which had settled over the capital city of the Kingdom of Hungary a week earlier and had since showed no sign of moving on. The chamber was sweltering. It was more likely however, that the low levels of both interest and attendance were due to the proposed legislation itself, which had absolutely no chance of securing passage.

Like its predecessors, the King's new federal plan called for Hungary to be divided into a number of new territorial states (eight, under the current scheme) based on ethnicity, each of which would have its own legislature, prime minister and other officers, while continuing to share the common Royal and Imperial Ministries of Finance, Foreign Affairs and War. In short, the Czechs, Croats, Poles, and so forth would each stand in relation to the whole of the Empire exactly as

Hungary and Austria did currently, as quasi-autonomous states. This federal model, based very loosely on the structure of the Swiss Confederation, had already been adopted in the Austrian half of the Dual Monarchy at the insistence of the Emperor, and over the objections of most of the German political parties, who stood to lose their control over the levers of power in the Empire.

However, the Emperor could and did wield far greater political clout in Cisleithania (the Austrian lands of the ancient Hapsburg dynasty), than he did in Hungary. The Hungarians had complete control of the reins of government in the Transleithania (otherwise known as the "Lands of the Crown of St. Stephen"), and did not have slightest intention of relinquishing them, whatever the details of the King's new plan of federation might be. Therefore, like the previous such proposals that came before the Diet on an annual basis, King Charles' new plan for sharing power with the various ethnic minorities under Hungarian rule was dead on arrival in Budapest, and everyone knew it. Even had Masayrk been a spellbinder along the lines of William Jennings Bryan, it would have changed nothing. The new Imperial proposal was not going to become law.

Suddenly, however, the day changed from utterly forgettable to one that no one who was present would ever forget. Mihaly Karolyi, the tall, dark-haired leader of the United Party of Independence and 1848 Party (which was generally known by the more convenient name of the "Karolyi Party"), the main opposition to the ruling Liberals, rose to his feet without asking for permission from the Speaker, and without preamble, began to berate the unsuspecting former professor of philosophy at the top of his lungs.

"Hungary is a great nation, single and indivisible, and I

defy you, the King or anyone else who would attempt to destroy it by dividing it up among a horde of lesser peoples!" he stormed at the astonished Czech delegate. Ignoring the excited gaveling and the demands for him to come to order by Prime Minister Tisza from high above the floor on the Government Bench, Karolyi ranted on. "I can no longer sit by and listen quietly as the enemies of my beloved Hungary attempt to destroy our great nation with their underhanded schemes. It is time, no, it is *past* time to sever the chains that tie us to the decaying Hapsburg Empire, time for an independent Greater Hungary to arise to greet its historic destiny, just as it is time for all true Magyar patriots to end their association with this lickspittle regime." Here he pointed theatrically at the Government Bench, so that no listener would be left in doubt as to which "lickspittle" regime he referred. "Our work begins here, today, *now!*"

With this, Karolyi turned and marched out of the great hall, sparing not a single backward glance for the pandemonium he had just caused. The other forty-odd members of his party followed their leader out of the Diet, doing their best to ignore the enraged catcalls and shouted insults showered upon them by their fellow deputies. It took Count Tisza fully thirty minutes to restore sufficient order to allow him to recess the session for the day.

It soon became apparent that Karolyi's dramatic speech and actions had constituted only the first phase of a larger plan. The walkout had come at 11:30. By 1:00, a huge crowd of his supporters had gathered in the great square outside the main entrance to the Parliament Building. The fact that so many thousands of his partisans were able to respond so quickly to an event that had occurred only ninety minutes earlier showed that Karolyi's actions on the floor of the legislature had not been the result of some sudden aberration.

Karolyi stood beneath the central arch at the top of the steps that led to the main entrance to the *Országház,* and breathed fire at his supporters. "Shall we bow down and become the slaves of lesser peoples, who would destroy our nation with their endless demands for national rights?" he demanded. *"No, no, never!"* the throng bellowed.

"Shall we become weaker, or shall we grow stronger?" he shouted, extending his arm and shaking his fist. Not surprisingly, his followers shouted, *"Stronger, stronger!"* Karolyi waited for the pandemonium to pass before he continued.

"Rather than being pulled apart into a dozen small, weak nations, shall we not share our glorious heritage and make new Magyars from Slovaks, Croats, Serbs, Romanians and the rest, until we build a Greater Hungary of twenty-five, thirty, even forty millions, so that the whole of Eastern Europe must follow where we lead?" Karolyi demanded.

This rhetorical query was greeted with a sustained, earsplitting paroxysm of cheers, and accompanied by the frenzied waving of a sea of Hungarian flags bearing the Kossuth coat of arms supported by archangels superimposed on horizontal bands of red, white and green.

From a balcony jutting out of an upper floor of the Parliament Building overlooking the square, Prime Minister Tisza looked on in amazement and disgust. He turned to his Interior Minister, Gabor Ugron, who stood at his side, and said, "I have no use for Karolyi or his politics, but until now I never suspected him to be mentally unbalanced. It's not as if the Diet was ever going to approve the King's new federal plan. He certainly knows that we..." by which he meant his ruling Liberal Party "...have no more use for it than he does. So why the all the nationalist ranting? What is he up to?"

"Will we allow Tisza and the rest of the Hapsburg's lackeys to steal our birthright?" Karolyi thundered. The crowd responded with shouts of "*No! No! Never!*" and "*Hungary will be free!*"

Ugron rubbed his forefinger over the bump on the bridge of his long nose. "I think, Your Excellency, that we must prepare for the possibility that he is planning to act in a manner consistent with his words," he said. "It is my belief that we shall soon be facing an attempt to overthrow the legally constituted government of the kingdom by armed force, and I suggest that we take immediate steps to meet this threat."

"A revolution? Do you really believe the situation is as serious as that, Gabor?" Tisza asked.

"Your Excellency, I strongly suggest that you contact Vienna to ask for the release of a division of cavalry to take the situation in hand before it becomes too big to control," Ungron said. "Meanwhile, I will call up every available policeman for emergency service. With your permission, I will issue orders to arrest Karolyi and the other leaders of his party. In addition, if this crowd does not disperse with the next hour, I will arrange for them to be sent on their way by mounted officers."

Tisza shook his head. "No. Absolutely not. You most emphatically do *not* have my permission for either action. An attack on a peaceful crowd by mounted police will simply add fuel to the fire, as would the arrest of their leader. Indeed, you could easily set off the very violence that we are trying to avoid. I am far from convinced that Karolyi is ready to attempt to bring down the government by means of a violent revolution. If that really is his plan, he will doubtless be looking for us to overreact, and thereby give the mob an incident to rally around. I will consult with Vienna, and we will await developments. You may call up additional police, and you will order your men to keep a close watch on Karolyi's partisans and make certain that no damage is done to innocent persons or property. But they are *not* to attack the crowd or attempt to take Karolyi or any members of his party into custody without my permission. Is that understood, Gabor?"

The Minister of the Interior nodded his head. "Understood, Your Excellency. May I be excused? I should return to my office immediately."

"Go," Tisza said. "We will speak again this evening."

He turned back to resume watching as Karolyi harangued the mass of humanity in the square with undiminished fervor. Could Ungron possibly be right? Was the mob below on the verge of breaking into the Parliament Building, overpowering the guards, seizing him and recreating the Defenestration of Prague by hurling the Emperor's minister out of a high window? He imagined for a moment what it would be like to be hurled ten meters down to the stones of the square below, and then he shook his head.

"No, Tisza, not today" he told himself. "This is not the day for you to give your life for your King." He turned his back on the square, Mihaly Karolyi, and his rapt auditors, and then walked back inside the building, pausing only to close the tall French doors behind him. He noted with some satisfaction that when they were shut, the doors dimmed the racket from outside considerably.

The Hungarian Parliament building, the *Országház*

CHAPTER FIVE
VIENNA, AUGUST 16, 1923

Had he been free to do what he wanted, Ray Swing would not at this moment be walking up the steps of the Schoenbrunn Palace for his scheduled interview with Emperor Charles. He would instead be on his way to Budapest, to witness and report on what was promising to be the biggest story of the year.

It was not that Swing thought an exclusive personal interview with the ruler of Austria-Hungary was less important than the events that were now unfolding in Budapest, even though that story rivaled in importance the recently ended Martinique affair, which had nearly touched off a war between the United States and Germany. Swing knew that the interview with Emperor Charles was an incredible opportunity for him, although he was still not certain how it had been arranged. But he did not think that, during the current crisis, with rumors of revolution and possible civil war in the air, the Emperor would have the time to meet him, either today, or for many days to come. Therefore, he was almost certainly wasting his time by coming to the palace, and he fully expected to be told that the interview would be postponed indefinitely. However, since he had heard nothing from the Austrians, he still had to go through the motions of showing up, even if it was to be told in person that he would not be able to see the Emperor today. A foreign correspondent did not stand up the Emperor of the Austria-Hungary, not unless he had given up all hope for career advancement.

Inside the Schoenbrunn he was met by an Imperial official, a man dressed in a uniform that would have been more appropriate for a major general than for a minor court functionary. The man very politely asked for Swing's identification and his authorization to enter the wing of the palace containing the Imperial apartments. He handed over his passport and the letter from the Emperor's secretary that contained the invitation to conduct the interview. As the man studied these documents and searched for his name in the gold-encrusted appointment book, Swing tried to estimate how long it would take him to return to his hotel, pack up, get to the *Ostbahnhof*, and catch a train to Budapest. Too long, he decided gloomily. All the excitement would probably be over by the time he got there.

His brooding was interrupted when the court official spoke after a surprisingly short delay. "Yes, Herr Swing, I see that your appointment is on the Emperor's schedule. Everything is in order. I will have someone take you up to see His Majesty immediately."

Swing was so surprised by this that he very nearly asked the man if there had been some kind of mistake. He was able to control this impulse with an effort, and instead said, "Oh… I mean, thank you."

The major general bowed in acknowledgement, and replied, "It was a pleasure to be of assistance to you, Herr Swing."

Another member of the palace staff, this one in a costume that would not have been out of place had it been worn by the ambassador from a small Central American republic. It featured a red sash running diagonally across the front of a black morning coat, with a monocle dangling from a chain anchored in the lapel, pencil-striped pants, and a decoration, in the form of a red and gold enameled starburst, on the breast of the coat. Swing speculated that the medal had been awarded for having the most brightly polished shoes for a week straight or some similar achievement.

He followed the man up a staircase decorated with an overhead fresco depicting a man in flapping, Classical draperies, a huge gout of flame, other figures on rearing horses, a throne, a crowd of people waving spears and swords over their heads, and a great deal more that he did not have time to puzzle out. He considered asking the Guatemalan Ambassador who was taking him to the Emperor what the picture was about, but then thought better of it.

At the top of the stairs, Swing was led into a parquet-floored room whose main feature was a series of large windows overlooking a courtyard. They passed into another room, this one also bare of furniture, but containing a half-dozen guardsmen in knee-length boots, dressed in red uniforms set off with gold braid, topped by gilded helmets. The men did not turn their heads or even shift their eyes to look at the two men passing through the room, and in fact did not appear to take notice of the existence of either man. From there, they entered another room, this one containing a billiards table and dominated by two huge paintings, both portraying large numbers of persons dressed in antique clothing gathering together for some unknown purpose (unknown to Swing, at least). This room had the distinction of being the first one in which he had seen any furniture.

Finally, they passed through an archway into a room paneled in burled walnut, gilded with Rococo decoration from floor to ceiling. There were two large mirrors, with elaborately carved gilt frames, several bow-legged armchairs painted gold, a marble topped table with intricately carved and gilded legs (the Austrians seemed enjoy gilding anything that would stand still long enough to have gold paint slapped on it), and at the far end of the room, a desk which stood out from all the other furnishings in that it was just plain wood, without any paint at all. Behind the desk engaged in writing, sat a slim, dark haired man with thin mustache, wearing a blue military jacket with gold buttons and a high collar. Standing beside him was another man, his short, dark hair slicked down and combed back over his head. Swing was immediately struck by the alert, intelligent expression on the face of the second man.

Swing's guide braced to attention, and announced, "Your Majesty, Mister Raymond Swing has arrived for his audience with you. Mr. Swing, I present His Imperial and Royal Majesty Charles the First, Emperor of Austria…"

"Yes, that's fine, thank you, Captain Dorner," the Emperor said in flawless English, looking up from his writing. "You may return to your duties."

He rose and offered his hand. "Thank you for coming, Mr. Swing. It is a pleasure to meet you. I have heard a great many things about you, all good. This is Prince Sixtus Bourbon, who serves as both my Prime Minister and my Interior Minister. He is also my brother-in-law. I hope you will not mind if he is present during the interview. It is largely because of him that I asked you to come to Vienna."

"It is a pleasure and an honor to meet Your Majesty…" Swing began.

"I think, since there are only the three of us present, we can dispense with the formalities," the Emperor said. "To begin with, I would prefer that you call me Karl, if you don't mind. Also, I think that we would all be more comfortable if we sat down."

"And I would rather you address me as 'Sixtus'," the Prince said. "I would like to say that I have been an admirer of your reporting since I first read your stories from the front lines in the Great War, Mr. Swing. I should also tell you that your current assignment was my idea, and that I helped to arrange for certain of Mr. Curtis's interview requests to be granted. A journalist of your experience is likely to have learned that altruism is not one of the major motivations for foreign policy, even in Austria. So at this point, you may be asking yourself: why?"

Swing nodded. Obviously, the Austrians wanted a *quid pro quo*; he was now about to find out the price for their unasked favors. "Actually, I'm not. I'm asking *you*: why?"

Sixtus' face clouded up, and he was on the verge of reminding the American that, informal meeting or not, he was in the presence of His Imperial and Royal Majesty, by the grace of God, Emperor of Austria, Apostolic King of Hungary, Bohemia, Dalmatia, Croatia *et cetera*, and that he would be well advised to conduct himself in an appropriate manner. Before he could reprimand the brash visitor, Karl chuckled and said, "Yes, I suppose you would probably get more information that way, Mr. Swing."

"I hope so," Swing replied. "By the way, I hope you both will call me 'Ray'. I'm a little uncomfortable addressing royalty by your first names while you are still calling me 'Mr. Swing'."

"Yes, of course, Ray," Karl said. "Now, to get back to your question, you may judge the importance I place on your presence here by the fact that the interview for your newspaper is taking place as scheduled in spite of recent events in Hungary. The storm in Budapest will soon blow over, and everything there will return to normal. But this meeting will have a profound effect on the future of the Empire. You must realize by now that the interview was merely a cover for some other purpose. In fact, you were brought here so that we can ask you to perform a diplomatic mission for my government."

Swing nodded. "I expected to be sent away this morning, and when I was brought up here instead, I had to wonder what could possibly be so important about an interview for a American newspaper."

"First, I must ask if you will swear to keep what you about to hear confidential, whatever your decision is about accepting this assignment," the Emperor continued. "We will be entrusting you with a state secret."

Swing considered for a moment, and then answered, "Yes, I can give you my word that I will keep whatever you tell me confidential. I'll be happy to put it in writing, if you like."

Karl exchanged a glance with his Prime Minister, who nodded, then back at Swing. "You have earned an enviable reputation for discretion, Ray. We believe that your word is quite sufficient. Sixtus, would you be good enough to explain the situation?"

"For various reasons, the Emperor has decided that the time has come for the Empire to end its association with Germany, and make new diplomatic arrangements with other powers before we are reduced to a vassal state by our powerful neighbor," Sixtus said. "However, there is the possibility that the government of Germany may not be prepared to accept such a change in our relationship gracefully."

"Do you think the Kaiser would invade the Empire if you try to pull out of the Triple Alliance?" Swing asked. "That seems a little extreme, even for Wilhelm."

"I would agree that an outright declaration of war is unlikely, although I would not necessarily rule out the possibility," Karl answered, "but the German political leadership is unpredictable, and almost any reaction short of war is a possibility. For example, they might send troops into our new Ukrainian province on the pretext of quelling ethnic disorder."

"In fact, Wilhelm has already issued thinly concealed threats to do something of this sort," Sixtus added. "But even if we assume that Germany does not pose a threat to the Empire in the short term, there remains the larger consideration of the future of Europe under German hegemony. I doubt that there is anyone more conscious of this threat than you are."

Swing nodded. For years he had been writing about the danger to world peace posed by a Germany newly engorged with land, resources and population all added as a result of the Great War of 1914. He had been largely ignored, a voice in the wilderness, at least in his own country, until the recently concluded Martinique Affair which seemed to have awakened the United States to the German threat. Now it appeared that the crisis had had something of the same effect in Vienna.

"Well, I can't argue with your reasoning," Swing said. "You want to get out from under German domination, and you need allies to at least make the Germans think twice before they decide to start carving off choice pieces of your territory. I can see that well enough. What I am not clear on is my role. Isn't this the sort of thing you pay your Foreign Minister to handle?"

"I have no doubt that your American State Department is completely clean of German agents," Karl began with an ironic smile, "but we in Austria are not so fortunate. If I were to assign this task to my Foreign Office, Kaiser Wilhelm would hear about it before any of my prospective allies. It is my hope that we will be able to keep the meeting of the future partners secret as long as possible, and thus limit the ability of Germany to interfere. It was my Prime Minister's suggestion that an American journalist such as you, ostensibly traveling about Europe to conduct a series of interviews, would be able to convey our proposals to the governments in question under circumstances that would not attract unwelcome attention. Given your well known views concerning Germany, we hoped that you would be willing to accept this task."

"I am honored that you would trust me, a stranger and a foreigner, with something as important as this," Swing answered. "If I hesitate, it's because I'm just a newspaperman, not a diplomat, and I am afraid that I might not be up to a job for which I have neither the training nor the experience."

"Suppose you let us be the judges of your qualifications, Ray?" asked Sixtus. "The Emperor and I believe you to the best man for the task. I will not say that the whole project will be called off if you refuse, but it would certainly be seriously delayed."

"We have not considered any alternative messenger," Karl said.

Swing wondered for an instant if that could possibly be true. Did the future of the Austro-Hungarian Empire really ride on the decision of the International Editor of the Philadelphia Inquirer? It was a little hard to credit. On the other hand, he could not help but be honored by the confidence the rulers of the Empire had in him. What finally decided him was the thought that among all the journalists in history, there were few, if any, who had given such an opportunity not merely to report on history but to be part of it.

"All right, gentleman, you have your messenger," he said. "What do you want me to do?"

CHAPTER SIX
BUDAPEST, AUGUST 18, 1923

As Mihaly Karolyi was about to open the door leading to his private office, he sensed a presence. Turning, he saw the familiar figure of his private secretary, Bela Molnar, trailing a respectful two paces behind him.

"Bela!" he barked, making the little man jump. "Leave me. I want some time alone. I will call you when I need you." Bela bobbed his head and hurried away without a word.

Karolyi instantly regretted snapping at his blameless secretary, and for an instant he considered calling him back and apologizing, before deciding that he could let it go until morning. He was in no mood to talk to anybody after just-completed meeting of his United Party of Independence and 1848 Party.

Before the meeting had even been officially opened, someone in the crowd (he could not see who it was) demanded to know exactly where he thought he was leading them. After that, the session degenerated into a free-for-all, with people leaping up to scream at the tops of their lungs that Karolyi should lead a mass march to storm Parliament, that the government Ministers be taken out, stood against a wall and shot, that he must declare the monarchy has been overthrown, declare Hungary to be a republic, and set up an interim revolutionary government, and so forth. At the same time, other members of the party demanded that he call for an end to the civil unrest, instruct the citizens of Budapest to resume their normal lives, and that he and the representatives of the party return to their seats in the Diet. Obviously, it was going to be impossible to satisfy all of these conflicting demands for action.

After two hours of bedlam, Karolyi ended the meeting by promising (bellowing at the top of his powerful lungs) to offer a comprehensive plan of action to the party within 24 hours, then, after quickly declaring the meeting adjourned, making his escape from the chaos of the hall as speedily as possible. He was exhausted, and had a brutal headache. Having promised the party faithful a new plan by the next day, he still had to formulate that plan, and he had not the slightest idea what he was going to tell them. What he really needed, he decided, was a little peace and quiet, so that he would have a chance to *think*.

He closed and locked the door of his office behind him, then turned and headed for the couch where he intended to lie on his back with his eyes closed until his head stopped throbbing. Before he reached his goal, he heard a voice say, "You have lost control of your party, Karolyi. What do you intend to do about it?"

He spun around to see a man seated at his desk. "How did you get in here?" Karolyi demanded doing his best to appear irate. "This is my private office. Who gave you permission…?" He ran down when he saw that his neither his words nor his tone were making the slightest impression on his visitor.

The man, known to Karolyi only as "Wolf", was unremarkable in appearance, with straight brown hair and a Chaplinesque postage-stamp mustache. Unremarkable, that is, until one got to the eyes. His gaze was intense, almost hypnotic, suggesting that he was a fanatic who was driven by some inner demon, although it was not clear to Karolyi exactly what he was fanatical about. He was not certain of the man's nationality, other than the fact that he was not a Hungarian. The way he spoke German hinted of a lower-middle class Austrian or Bavarian origin. What he did know was that Wolf, or whatever his name was, made him uncomfortable. He longed to throw the fellow out of his office, but under the circumstances he had little choice but to at least treat him with basic civility.

Wolf stood and approached. "Well, Karolyi?" he asked. "Your party is falling to pieces around you. Your people demand a strong hand to guide them and cannot make up your mind what to do. This is the moment of truth. How will you respond?"

Karolyi waved his hands in the air. "What am I supposed to do? Tisza was supposed to be stampeded into ordering the police to fire into the crowds or to make mass arrests, or do *something*, anything, to create an incident for us to stir up the mob with, but he isn't cooperating and my people are losing interest."

"Call for a general strike," Wolf suggested. "Your party controls some of the big trade unions. Tell them to shut down the city."

Karolyi shook his head. The man understood almost nothing of political realities in Budapest. "It wouldn't work. The Liberals have as many trade unions as we do, including the most important one for a general strike, the transport workers. The strike would fizzle out, and all we would do is make a display of our true weakness."

"Then arm your followers and lead them on a march to the Diet," Wolf said. "Batter down the doors, arrest Tisza and his ministers at the point of a gun, and stage a *putsch*. Power belongs to those who are bold enough to seize it!" Wolf gestured ferociously with his fists as he spoke, as if he imagined himself inspiring a great crowd with his words.

Karolyi sank down to the couch, staring at the man in dismay. "Parliament Square is guarded by lines of armed police. Just how do you suggest that I persuade my people to commit high treason and hurl themselves on their guns? What great cause shall move them to sacrifice their lives at my prompting?" he asked sarcastically.

"For the only cause with any meaning: for your *volk*, for the racial destiny of your people," Wolf answered. "My race has been defeated in Austria, and is doomed to be submerged in a sea of subhuman Czechs, Slovaks, Poles, Croats and, worst of all, the purveyors of filth and venereal disease, the vile Jews. Your Magyars still have a chance to save themselves, but they must have a leader who can inspire them with this great cause. Go!" he said, pointing dramatically. "Lead your people on to greatness!"

Karolyi's expression was that of a man who has just seen something unpleasant crawl out from under a rock. He was beginning to understand the nature of the demon that drove this Wolf, and the knowledge made him slightly ill. Karolyi believed wholeheartedly in the superiority of Magyar culture, but he thought racism, especially Wolf's brand of primitive anti-Semitism, was barbaric, stupid and sickening. *Anyone* had the potential to be a good Magyar. It had nothing to do with who your parents were or what religion you followed. Indeed, rather than being a threat to the nation, the Jews could be pointed to as the model for other ethnic minorities to follow. Instead of resisting assimilation, they embraced it, and in a single generation many of the Jews who had fled persecution in Russia and emigrated to the Dual Monarchy had become good, loyal citizens of the Kingdom. Their children were indistinguishable from other Magyars, as far as Karolyi was concerned. He certainly trusted any of the many Hungarian Jews he called friends more than he did this Wolf character.

"I have taken your employer's thirty pieces of silver and I have done what was required of me in return because, whatever his motives may be, I will take any aid that will help to create an independent Hungarian nation," Karolyi replied. "But I have never promised to stick my head into the noose on behalf of Kaiser Wilhelm, and I have not the slightest intention of doing so now."

Wolf's features hardened in anger. He glared at the other man. "On what basis do you conclude that I am employed by the German Empire?" he demanded.

The Hungarian snorted. "Who else stands to gain so much from a disruption of the Empire? It is hardly a secret that the Kaiser has been eyeing the new Polish and Ukrainian lands the Empire added after the war. A massive civil disturbance followed by rioting and other disorders would make an excellent pretext for German troops to occupy those territories, temporarily and only to keep order, of course. After that, I have no doubt that it would not be difficult to find excellent reasons for remaining on a permanent basis. The scheme is consistent with the usual German methods: which is to say, approximately as subtle as a meat-axe," he said. "In any case, you must realize by now that you have been watched by my people since the first day you made contact with me. After you have been observed meeting covertly with the most notorious German *agents-provocateur* in Hungary, it would not be very difficult to guess who you were acting for."

Wolf swept a dismissive hand through the air. "All of that is meaningless. The name of my employer is irrelevant. The only thing that matters now is *action*. The whole rotten,

Jew-infested Imperial structure is ready to collapse from the first solid push. Will you be the one to make it, or will it be left to another, a man with the courage to do what is necessary?"

Karolyi ignored the taunt, and stretched out full length on the sofa, resting his head on a padded arm. "I'll let you know what I decide in the morning," he said wearily. "Now go away, Wolf." He closed his eyes and drifted off into the dark sea of sleep.

Mihaly Karolyi by Cecile Tormay

CHAPTER SEVEN
VIENNA, AUGUST 19, 1923

Ray Swing looked at the girl sitting across the table from him, then down at the sheet of paper he held in his hand, then back up at the girl again. She was stunningly attractive, with a peaches-and-cream complexion that contrasted dramatically with her jet-black hair that framed her face and was cut even with her jaw-line, in the currently fashionable style. With features of classical beauty and a body to match, Swing would have instantly believed her if she had claimed to be a high-fashion model or an actress. But he was having a hard time accepting the story she was telling him.

"I still don't understand how you were hired, or rather why," he said. "Suppose you go over it for me again, Miss..." He glanced down at the letter of introduction from John Curtis that she had handed him, "...Collins."

"Of course, Mr. Swing," she said. "As I said before, I am an American stringer..." here she held up a Speed Graphic for his scrutiny, which looked to the skeptical Swing as if it had just been taken from its original box that day, to demonstrate her *bona fides*, "... currently working out of Vienna. Yesterday, I received the letter you are holding in your hand from Mr. John Curtis in Philadelphia. He is the Managing Editor of the ..."

"Yes, I know the name of my boss," Swing interrupted impatiently. "Just get on with it."

"Oh yes, I suppose you would," Collins said. "Well,

anyway, Mr. Curtis asked me if I would be available to travel with you, to take photographs of your interview subjects to run with the series when it is published in the *Inquirer*, just as the letter states. I agreed, and… that's about it, I suppose."

"But…" Swing began, then stopped. He could understand Curtis having a photographer assigned to the story (although not why had it only occurred to him at this late date), but it was far from clear to him why he had selected a girl he had never heard of (in fact, he was not aware of the existence of another female news photographer) over dozens of seasoned professional cameramen, any of whom would have jumped at such an assignment. The letter seemed to be authentic, written as it was in Curtis's distinctive flowing script (or an excellent imitation thereof). In any case, Swing had received a telegram from Curtis confirming the assignment of his new camera… man… (What was the right word? Camerawoman?) just a few hours earlier. Whatever was going on, his editor evidently was involved in and approved of it. Nonetheless, there was definitely something fishy about the whole affair.

"What sort of experience do you have in the newspaper business, Miss Collins?" he asked.

"Oh, please call me Kate," she said, "since we're going to be working together. May I call you Ray?"

"Yes, sure, Kate," Swing said. "So, how long have you been working over here? What papers did you work for back home?" he persisted.

"I haven't actually done any professional photography in the United States," she admitted. "I've been freelancing for some small magazines here in Europe over the last few years, but not anything very important, like the stories you've covered," she added, managing to combine modesty, flattery and vagueness in a single sentence.

"Where are you from originally?" Swing asked.

"I grew up in Cincinnati," she said.

"I haven't been there for ten years, at least," Swing said. "Is Everett's Steak House over on Dermott Street still as good as it was back in the old days? They used to say that they served the best beefsteak in the country, and they probably did."

The girl hesitated almost imperceptibly before answering. "Oh yes, my father took us there a several times, on special occasions. The last time was when I graduated from high school. The food is still excellent."

Swing nodded, his suspicions confirmed. This Kate Collins (which probably was not her real name), was no more a native of Cincinnati than Swing was the heir to the Holy Roman Empire. "Really? That's a little difficult to believe, since I just invented both Everett's and Dermott Street."

The girl flushed, whether in anger or embarrassment he could not tell. She seemed about to say something, then faltered. Before she could make up her mind what to say, Swing asked, "So, why don't you drop the play-acting and tell me who you really are and why you're pretending to be a freelance photographer?"

She smiled ruefully and shook her head. "I *told* them you would never believe that foolish cover story," she said. "I wanted to simply tell you the truth in the first place."

"That being...?" Swing prompted.

"My real name is Christina Dietrichstein, and I am employed the Ministry of the Interior as an agent of the *Kaiserlich und Königlich Evidenzbureau*, which is..." she said.

"Which is the Imperial spy service," Swing finished for her.

"The Intelligence Bureau, yes," she nodded. "The Interior Minister, Prince Parma Bourbon, personally assigned me to accompany you on your travels for your protection from…"

"Just what are you supposed to protect me from?" Swing broke in again. "Who does the Prince imagine might wish to do me harm?"

"You must realize that there would be some element of danger for you personally, when you agreed to undertake a secret diplomatic mission for the Austrian government. There is always the possibility that agents of unfriendly powers might learn the real reason for your mission, and try to keep you from completing it," she answered. "Or they may wish to learn about what you are doing, and create inconveniences for you in their attempts to obtain information."

"What sort of 'inconveniences' does he expect these imaginary agents to cause for me?" Swing demanded.

"I do not think he is not *expecting* anything in particular," Christina said. "I believe that he merely wishes to be prepared for the possibility."

"Possibility of *what*?" he persisted. "Somebody sticking a knife in my ribs in a dark alley, or snatching me off the street at midnight?" he asked, proposing the most melodramatic and implausible possibilities he could think of to ridicule the idea.

Her response was not what he expected. "One never knows, Mr. Swing," she said seriously. "That is precisely the reason I was chosen to watch over you."

" 'Ray', please. You can still call me Ray, even if you aren't a real photographer," he said. "All right, let's suppose I am being followed around by mysterious spies in trench coats who plan to kidnap me and torture me for my secrets. Why pick *you* as my bodyguard? No offense intended, Miss

Dietrichstein... Christina," he amended, "but how much safer would I be with you guarding me than I would be traveling on my own?"

"No offense taken, Ray," she answered, smiling. "In fact, my superiors are counting on any hostile agents to share your assumption that as a weak, useless female I can safely be disregarded." She made a slight movement with her right hand, there was a *thong!* and suddenly a black-handled six-inch steel blade was quivering in Swing's chair, six inches away from his right ear. His head snapped to the right to look at the knife, then back at the Austrian agent. She now held a small silver automatic pistol in her left hand that was trained on his sternum. "It is hoped that the hostile operatives, if any, may therefore miscalculate by leaving me out of their plans."

"Ahh, I see," he said thoughtfully, his eyes fixed on the gun, which still pointed unwaveringly at his breastbone. "I think that all my questions have been answered for the time being, so maybe you can put your piece away for a while."

"Oh yes, sorry," she said apologetically, slipping the weapon into a fold in her jacket.

With some effort, Swing tugged the knife out of the wood of the chair back, and returned it to his lovely (and evidently lethal) companion. "We have a train to catch at five o'clock..." the next stop on Swing's itinerary was Rome, where he was to interview Prime Minister Giovanni Giolitti, "...so we have a couple of hours to work on your impression of a photographer. I am guessing that you are not an expert with that fancy camera you have there, so let me give you a few pointers. Then maybe, just *maybe*, somebody might mistake you for an actual freelancer. I've never been a photographer myself, but I've worked with plenty of good ones over the years."

Privately, he thought that she was far too glamorous for the part, and would fool no one. On the other hand, Christina's fabulous looks would probably make her the center of attention of any male who was in the same room as her, so that it was possible Swing would go completely unnoticed while in her company.

"Thank you, Ray," she said. She awkwardly lifted the bulky camera from the table.

"No, no," he admonished. "A real photographer would never hold her camera like that. First, you grab the handle on top..."

Speed Graphic "Top Handle"

CHAPTER EIGHT
BUDAPEST, AUGUST 23, 1923

In the end, Mihaly Karolyi was completely unprepared when the match that set the revolution ablaze was struck. But then, so was everyone else.

After much agonizing, he had had finally decided to make one last attempt to force the Tisza government to resign, even though he personally had little faith in the plan's prospects for success. He called for a mass rally of all patriotic Hungarians, of all parties, to gather together and march through the streets to Parliament Square, where they would present a petition demanding Tisza and his ministry to step down. This, Karolyi told his supporters, would be the beginning of a new political organization that would replace Tisza's Liberal Party and begin the process of creating a renewed free and independent Hungary – the kind of party he envisioned would resemble the opposition Party of National Renewal in Russia, or Clemenceau's National Radical Party in France, offering the combined appeals of social welfare programs for the working classes and patriotic nationalism for the conservative voters.

Karolyi did not expect his new plan to drive out the government, nor did he harbor any real hope for his proposed new party. This was largely because of his understanding of Hungarian politics. He had no reason to think that any of his rivals would agree to merge their parties together under his leadership, no matter what the potential benefits might be. This was understandable: had he been in their shoes, he would not have agreed to place himself and his people under their authority under any circumstances. His trust in his political opponents was practically non-existent, and he knew that the converse was true.

However, he was gratified at the popular reception to his call for the anti-government rally and march. The public response was so great that Karolyi's political rivals were forced to pretend that they too were enthusiastic about joining the event, although none of them went so far as to make a commitment to join his proposed new umbrella political party. Tens of thousands of Hungarians from across the political spectrum, including contingents from the Tisza's own Liberal Party, flooded into the capital from the countryside to join the swelling crowds in the city. Among them were obscure groups that Karolyi had scarcely ever heard of before.

Among the latter was one calling itself the Sons of Arpad, a recently formed veteran's organization which was named after a semi-legendary 9th century figure, supposedly the first ruler of the Magyar tribes. The founder and leader of the group was a 55 year-old former naval officer named Miklos Horthy, who was known to his followers more familiarly as Captain Horthy. Up to now, the Sons of Arpad had shown interest only in the limited area of soldiers' and sailors' pensions, and this rally was their political coming-out party.

The contingent of the Sons of Arpad arrived in a long column, marching in company-sized formations under the direction of 'officers'. They were dressed in uniforms consisting of green trousers, white shirts and red caps, and altogether were rather too military in appearance for Karolyi's comfort. The men were all armed with either pistols or mean-looking truncheons hanging from their white belts, in spite of Karolyi's insistence that the marchers be unarmed, as proof of their peaceful intentions. (This requirement had earned a magnificent sneer from Wolf when he heard it).

Karolyi at first was inclined to forbid the Sons of Arpad from participating as long as they were carrying weapons. Captain Horthy explained that the weapons were necessary in the event that the police went wild and started massacring the crowd. He promised that his men, veterans all, had no intention of causing trouble, were under strict discipline, and would act only in an emergency, and then only to the extent needed to defend their fellow participants in the rally, which included many thousands of the elderly, women and children. These arguments won over most of the leaders of the other parties and, finally, a reluctant Karolyi.

The march through the streets of Pest to Parliament Square went well at first, although the crowds were so large that it took more than two hours longer than was originally planned. Although the marchers were clearly enthusiastic for their cause, they were in a cheerful, even festive, mood. Thousands of Hungarian flags were in evidence, from handkerchief-sized ones on tiny wooden sticks in the hands of children who waved them excitedly, to the big two-meter long banners mounted on long wooden staffs carried by the Sons of Arpad, lending color to the holiday-like atmosphere. Karolyi, standing on the temporary speaker's platform, watching the crowds pour into Parliament Square, could detect no sign of violence in the happy throng.

As had been the case since the day Karolyi had staged his party's walkout from the Diet, a double line of state police on foot backed by another line of mounted officers along the western side of the plaza, guarding the main entrance of the imposing *Országház*, home of the Kingdom's government. The crowd was so huge that many thousands of hopeful participants could not even enter the square and were condemned to catch only distant glimpses of the event from the streets leading up to the Square.

Although afterwards there were many conflicting claims from eyewitnesses, no investigation was ever able to conclusively prove exactly how it started. Witnesses agree that the police grew conspicuously tense when the armed formations of the Sons of Arpad marched into position, at the very front of the Square, close to the police lines. The first speaker of the event (an otherwise undistinguished conservative politician by the name of Laszlo Lukacs) was just beginning his remarks when the sound of at least one gunshot rang out. It came from the direction of the southwestern corner of the Square, where the Sons of Arpad were stationed, but whether a member of that paramilitary group fired the first shot, no one could say.

Some survivors claimed that immediately after the initial shot or shots, a machine gun began to fire, but this is almost certainly not correct, as no weapon of this kind was ever seen or recovered after the fighting. What they probably heard was the very rapid discharge of police weapons, which could have been mistaken for the chatter of a machine gun by someone who had never heard one before. Many witnesses swore that there was also an explosion, which sounded like a bomb or grenade of some kind, but this is disputed. The only thing that everyone who was present near the front of the Square agrees on is that seconds after the first discharge, the police leveled their rifles and side arms at the crowd, and began firing with deadly intent and effect, and that the Sons of Arpad started shooting back at the state police with an equally murderous purpose.

Panic began in the front rows of the crowd, and only

gradually spread back through the immense throng, as the screams of the wounded cut through the slogan-chanting mass. In the front of the crowd, dozens of protestors crumpled to lie on the pavement, writhing and crying out for help amid spreading pools of blood. Among countless scenes of horror, many of the survivors recall a dark-haired woman holding aloft a boy of perhaps three with a bullet hole drilled through his forehead, shrieking at the police and making no attempt to save herself, until she too was gunned down.

The crowd reacted in two distinct ways to the police gunfire. On one hand, most of the crowd, who were unarmed and unprepared for violence, did everything in their power to escape the carnage, pushing, shoving and running madly away from the shooting, heedless of those who had fallen under their feet. This panicked stampede actually resulted in more casualties than did the shooting. Out of the 567 people killed on Budapest's infamous Bloody Thursday, fewer than a third (181) were victims of gunshot wounds. The remainder succumbed to injuries sustained as a result of being trampled by fear-crazed mob's attempt to escape from the gunfire. In addition, an unknown number of the participants, several thousand at least, suffered wounds ranging from cracked skulls and broken ribs to mashed fingers and sprained ankles, all consistent with being battered and crushed under the feet of their fellows.

On the other hand, thousands of the participants in the rally had served in the Royal and Imperial Army in the Great War, and they were not inclined to run away at the sight of blood, especially when the blood was that of their neighbors and loved ones. On the contrary, many of these men were enraged by the slaughter of unarmed civilians by the state police, particularly as many of the slain were women, children and old people. Moreover, they were heartened by the resistance of Captain Horthy's disciplined Sons of Arpad. They were aware that they had an overwhelming numerical superiority over the roughly 250 police lining the Square in front of the Parliament Building. Shouting encouragement to each other, the men gathered together in groups, and in the face of point-blank fire, charged the police lines and overran them. They were aided by the fact that the many of the police were not able to concentrate their weapons on them, as they were already engaged in a firefight with the Sons of Arpad.

Only seconds after the assault began, the attackers were in among the police lines, and after that the fighting was over in less than a minute. The foot patrolmen were beaten to death with fists or improvised weapons, stamped underfoot, or else shot with guns seized from their colleagues or picked from the ground, while the mounted police were dragged from their horses and dispatched with fists, boots and knives. The only surviving police were the few who threw down their weapons and ran as soon as they saw the charge beginning to take shape.

Karolyi had been sitting in a folding chair on the speaker's stand looking over his speech when the gunfire broke out. He stared for a few seconds, watching in disbelief as his 'peaceful' rally degenerated into a carnival of slaughter. He was snapped out of his trance when a bullet slammed into a right-wing politician seated beside him on the stand. There was a wet *thump*! and the man toppled over dead at Karolyi's feet. Looking around, he suddenly realized how dangerous his exposed position was. He threw himself flat on the platform, and then crawled as rapidly as possible to the front, which was the side farthest away from the gunfire, and dropped to the ground. When he heard the roar made by the veterans attacking the police, he peeked out around the corner of the platform just in time to witness the state police being torn to pieces by the wrathful mob.

As suddenly as it started, the shooting stopped. The air was filled with the moans of the wounded and the cries of weeping women. The men who had stormed the police lines paused, milling about uncertainly, while officers of the Sons of Arpad began reorganizing their men and assigning them to help the wounded. Karolyi stood up slowly, stunned by the scope of the massacre. The sight of the hundreds of dead and wounded citizens of all ages and both sexes lying in their blood around the Parliament Square was like a scene from a nightmare.

"God help me, this is all my fault," he whispered. He buried his face in his hands. An overwhelming, almost physical sense of guilt tore at him. He was sure that he would never be able to forgive himself for being the cause of this terrible tragedy. He wept, his shoulders shaking with his sobs.

A familiar and unwelcome voice cut into his grieving. "The moment has struck! Now is the time to act!" it said.

He opened his eyes and brusquely wiped the tears away with his hands. Standing at his side was Wolf, his eyes gleaming with excitement. "You have been given a priceless gift, and you must use it," he urged. He gestured at the men who had just destroyed the state policemen and Horthy's Sons of Arpad. "They require only a leader, and they will follow the first man who speaks up. Take them in there," he pointed at the Parliament Building. "Arrest Tisza and his ministers, and announce the birth of a new, independent Hungary! You have only to stretch out your hand and power will drop into it like a ripe fruit!"

Karolyi stared at the man beside him. In an instant, his

emotions veered from near-suicidal despair to an almost homicidal rage. Wolf considered this massacre of innocents to be... what? A golden opportunity? A priceless gift from the gods?

"*Shut up! Shut up! Shut the hell up!*" he shrieked at the German agent, spittle flying from his lips. Wolf hastily backed away from the raving madman.

Somehow, Karolyi found himself standing back on the speaker's platform (he had no memory of going back there). His eardrums were assaulted by a man's voice. The speaker had the loudest unamplified voice he had ever heard. It took a second or two for him to realize that it was he, Karolyi, who was speaking

"*Murderers!*" he howled. Every living person in the square, with the exception of the most severely wounded, looked up, startled.

The words spilled from Karolyi's mouth without his volition. "The men who gave the orders to kill us, to murder our wives and our daughters, to slaughter our sons and brothers, they are in there!" He pointed at the Parliament. "The butchers Tisza, Ungron and the others are hiding in that building! Will we let them escape punishment for their crimes?"

One tiny corner of Karolyi's mind was still rational. It whispered that he was talking nonsense. It was certain that neither the Prime Minister nor the Minister of the Interior, nor indeed anyone in the government had ordered this massacre, and the voice reminded him that no one was more responsible for what had happened here than Karolyi himself. He savagely suppressed the voice, and allowed unreasoning rage to swallow him.

A low, savage growling noise rose from the remaining

crowd, mixed with cries of "*No! No!*"

"They do not deserve trials! They should be given the same chance they gave our wives and children. They should be lined up against a wall and *shot*! We must take them now, before they escape from justice!" Karolyi shrieked. "I am going in there to capture the criminals. Is anyone with me?" He jumped down from the platform and began to walk towards the main entrance to the building, not even looking back to see if anyone was following him.

There were many cries of "*Kill them!*" "*Shoot the bastards!*" and so forth, as thousands of men gathered on either side and behind Karolyi. Most of them were still weaponless, but many had armed themselves with rifles or handguns they had taken from the bodies of the slain state policemen.

Captain Horthy appeared at Karolyi's side, with his Sons of Arpad marching behind him. "I place myself and my men under your orders until this government of murderers is brought down," he said.

Karolyi hardly noticed the man. All of his attention was fixed on the remaining handful of police who watched in growing terror as the vengeful mob approached the doors of the Parliament Building they were assigned to guard. They had witnessed the fate of their now-deceased colleagues, and unsurprisingly, had no desire to share it. Someone in the mob fired his pistol and, as if this was a signal, the policemen fled, scattering to either side of the Parliament Building, and then running west towards the Danube.

As the mob wrenched open the doors and ran through the halls of the seat of government of the Kingdom of Hungary, screaming for blood, another rational thought struggled up through the sea of primitive emotions which at that moment ruled Karolyi.

No matter how this turns out, at least Kaiser Wilhelm will be pleased, he thought.

Budapest Parliament interior by Karelj

CHAPTER NINE
PARIS, AUGUST 25, 1923

Ray Swing and Christina Dietrichstein sat in an undistinguished Left Bank café eating what passed for breakfast in France, which in that non-breakfast-eating land meant coffee and rolls. They were passing the time before an afternoon meeting with Edouard Herriot, who was the current Premier and Foreign Minister of the French Republic. Swing was reading the *Paris Herald's* account of the recent and startling events of what the newspapers were calling "Bloody Thursday" in Budapest. His photographer/bodyguard had a vile French cigarette hanging from the corner of her mouth as she pretended to make adjustments to her camera.

"The Emperor and Prince Sixtus seemed to have underestimated the seriousness of the Hungarian crisis," Swing remarked, his face hidden from his companion by the pages of the newspaper. "I don't think they expected Tisza and his Interior Minister to be dragged out of the Diet at gunpoint and executed, or an independent Hungarian Republic to be declared. There may not even be an Imperial representative at this conference we're trying to arrange for your Emperor, assuming there ever is one, because there may be no Austro-Hungarian Empire by then. Ironic, don't you think?" he asked.

As he expected, she did not evince even the slightest interest in the news that her nation was tottering on the edge of the abyss of civil war and possible disintegration. Although the Austrian agent was both beautiful and intelligent, she left much to be desired as a traveling companion, in Swing's opinion. She was interested in only one thing, to the exclusion of all else: her mission. It seemed that nothing, not even the most startling news, could distract her from her single-minded concentration on her assignment.

"Our new friends have found us again," Christina said, squeezing the words out of one corner of her mouth, while she continued to retain the cigarette pinched between her lips on the other side. "Don't look," she said quickly, as he automatically began to lower his paper. "They're sitting behind me to the left, at a place halfway down the block on the other side of the street."

She had originally spotted the two men following them in Rome, four days earlier. When she later told Swing about the tail in his hotel room, she added that she felt reasonably certain that whoever they were working for did not consider the reporter a very high-priority target.

"You're saying that the fact that two foreign agents are following me means that whoever sent them doesn't think I'm doing anything important?" he demanded. "Explain that, if you will."

"If somebody actually thought you were engaged in a significant mission, they would have sent *competent* operatives out to follow you," she said. "But if it was just a routine job, to keep you under observation and see where you go, I suppose their boss might think that these two…" she paused, searching for an appropriately scathing term, then shook her head as if she was unable to come up with one, and finished "…men would be good enough."

"What exactly leads you to believe that they're following me, anyway?" Swing asked skeptically.

"Oh, that was easy enough to see," she said. "I spotted

them right away in that *trattoria* where we had dinner. They stuck out like a pair of sore thumbs."

"I didn't notice them," Swing said. "What was so obvious about them?"

"A lot of little things," she began. "First of all…" she stopped. "It doesn't really matter. Once I suspected them, I confirmed it then and there. Do you remember when I asked you to go up to the register to buy me a pack of cigarettes?"

"Yeah, I remember. So what?" he replied.

"As soon as you left the table, I got up and went to *le signore*, and they showed themselves," she said.

"How? Did they hold up their 'foreign spy' cards for you?" Swing asked sarcastically.

"Almost," she answered. "I walked very slowly across the room, and every man in that restaurant stared at me, even the ones having dinner with their wives or girlfriends. Every man but those two: they never took their eyes off you. They probably were watching in case the counter-man slipped you a secret message along with the packet of cigarettes."

The Austrian agent was obviously more than competent at her work, but by the time they reached Paris after a solid week of being made to feel like a bumbling amateur, Swing was growing weary of her routine displays of professional expertise. He was beginning to feel as if he was playing the part of the slow-witted Watson to her brilliant Sherlock Holmes, and he did not particularly care for it. "Well, how do you know where they are, if they're behind you?" he grumbled.

She made a tiny motion of her head over her left shoulder. There was a large mirror in the display window of a dress shop located next to the café. "I saw their reflections when they sat down a few minutes ago. I think I may have to do something about those two. I have a feeling that they are not happy with what they are learning from just following you, and are preparing to investigate more..." she paused, "...energetically, shall we say?"

Swing had learned not to challenge Christina on her hunches and thereby run the risk of being handed another "elementary, my dear Watson." Instead, he asked, "What did you have in mind?"

"There are any number of ways that I could easily kill both of them, and dispose of the bodies so that it could never be connected to us," she said matter-of-factly, as if she were discussing the train schedule.

Swing suppressed a shudder at the cold-blooded way she talked about murdering two strangers, men that she only *suspected* were foreign agents. "I'm sure you could, but don't you think that might be a little counter-productive?"

She frowned. "How do you mean?"

"It's just possible that their bosses would get suspicious if the two men assigned to follow me suddenly turned up dead or suddenly stopped reporting in, don't you think?" Swing asked. "The idea is to remain *in*conspicuous, and your plan may not be the best way doing that," he said with considerable understatement.

Christina thought about it, and then nodded. "You have a point," she admitted.

"What we really want to do is satisfy them that I am exactly what I appear to be: a reporter going about his business," Swing said. "Then they should lose interest in me and go off to follow some other unfortunate soul around Europe."

"Agreed," she said. "You have a plan, I suppose?"

He removed his glasses, and held them up in front of his face to polish them with his handkerchief, and not coincidently hiding a smile of satisfaction. He replaced his glasses and leaned forward across the table. "As a matter of fact, I do. After the interview with Herriot..." he began.

The meeting with the French Premier went well, once M. Herriot had satisfied himself that the Austrian feeler was genuine and not some kind of trick. He took his time studying the letter introducing Swing, which was written in the Emperor's own hand and which explained the true purpose of the meeting. After that, he spent the next hour looking over Karl's treaty proposal, grilling Swing about the details and asking the American his opinion of the sincerity of the Austrians.

" 'The purpose of the alliance will be to maintain peace by forming a common front of like-minded Powers against any aggressor nations, and will be open to any nation who wishes to join for this purpose'," Herriot read aloud. "Each member shall be obligated to declare war on any aggressor state in the event of an attack on any member state by an non-member state'."

He looked up. "Do you think Wilhelm will want to sign on?" Herriot asked ironically. "According to him, all Germany wants is peace."

"Yes, a piece of Poland, a piece of Galicia, and a piece of the Ukraine," the journalist said. Both men had read the statement that afternoon out of Berlin, announcing that units of the German Army would be occupying southern Poland, Ruthenia, and parts of the Ukraine belonging to Austria-Hungary to "protect lives and property of German citizens", "suppress dangerous rioting by radicals and Bolsheviks", and to "maintain order until such time as the Government of

Austria-Hungary is able to restore effective administration" over the troubled areas.

"Just so," agreed the French Premier. "The Emperor desires to convene this conference at the beginning of October. But will he still be ruling a Great Power by then, or will there be nothing remaining but bits and pieces of his Empire a month from now?"

Swing had signed on as Karl's messenger, not his salesman, but he had gradually come to take a strong personal interest in the successful outcome of his mission. He therefore came to the Karl's defense. "I think, Monsieur Herriot, that at the very least the Austrian part of the Empire will remain intact. The Emperor's internal reforms have strengthened it enough to withstand the current stress. As a matter of fact, I wonder if Austria would not be better off without the dead weight of Hungary blocking every attempt at reform, every effort to modernize the country and put it on a more stable basis."

"That remains to be seen," Herriot said noncommittally. "In any event, you may assure the Emperor that France will not hesitate to ally herself with anyone who desires to restrain..." he hesitated for a fraction of a second, almost saying "Germany", before finishing "...aggressor nations."

Swing completed the meeting by interviewing the Premier about the current political situation in France and the prospects for his National Radical Party in the coming elections for his Inquirer piece, and then brought Christina in to take a few pictures.

"How did it go?" she asked as they descended the steps of the Assemblée Nationale into the Place de la Concorde.

Swing glanced at his companion in surprise at her apparent newly developed interest in politics, then saw from her expression that this was a mere politeness. "Oh, about as expected, I guess," he answered. "It's not as if the French have any better offers, after all."

She nodded absently, her attention having already moved on. "There they are," she said, shifting her eyes slightly to indicate the direction of their two shadows.

"Yeah, I saw them as soon as we came outside," Swing answered. "Are you ready?"

"As soon as they come into earshot," she said.

The agents were lounging on adjoining benches, pretending to read newspapers as they approached. Suddenly, Christina stopped in her tracks and seized the arm of Swing's jacket.

"No, Raymond, *no!*" she exclaimed. "You can't go to bed early *again* tonight. We're in Paris, *Paris*, for God's sake, and you just *have* to take me out tonight. We've both been working so *hard*, and we deserve to have a little *fun*."

All in all, she did a very credible imitation of a whining, empty-headed American flapper. Swing, who up until that moment had not been altogether confident that her thespian skills were up to the demands of the part, was impressed. He concentrated on his role, as an all-work, no-play journalist. (In fact, he had never met such a specimen, and he seriously doubted if one existed.)

"We are in Paris on an assignment, Miss Collins, in case you have forgotten," he said sternly. "The *Inquirer* didn't send us here to have *fun*," he said, lending derisive emphasis to the word. "They sent us to do a job."

"But we *completed* the assignment, Raymond," she wheedled authentically, "and we're on our *own* time now. Would it *kill* you to take me out for a few drinks just one night?"

Swing rolled his eyes in exasperation, then, with apparent bad grace, gave in. "All right. After I finish writing up the Herriot interview, there's no harm in going out for a few hours, I suppose," he said.

Christina shouted, "Oh, thank you, Raymond!" She wrapped both arms around his neck and planted an enthusiastic-seeming kiss on the surprised reporter's lips. They went off together, doing their best to give the impression that they had not even seen the two men who sat a few feet away, their heads buried in their newspapers.

After they had left the Place de la Concorde far behind, Swing asked, "Do you think they suspected anything?"

She smiled and shook her head. "Not a chance. The only thing I'm afraid of is that they're not smart enough to pick up the hint. Maybe I should have said..." here she began speaking again in her silly flapper voice "... 'But *Raymond*, we'll be out of our hotel rooms for *hours*. Do you think our *things* will be safe?' just to be sure."

Swing could not restrain a snort of laughter. "Let's hope it wasn't necessary to make it quite so obvious," he said.

Two hours later, an American reporter and his escort stepped out of the Hotel D'Aubusson into the Rue Dauphine, evidently beginning a night in the City of Light. A hundred feet away, pretending to study a menu posted in the window of a café, was a man they had last seen in the afternoon, sitting on a park bench in the Place de la Concorde. The couple turned to walk down the narrow street in the opposite direction of the menu-reader, and strolled along at an unhurried pace until they turned right on the Rue de Buci.

"How long do you think they'll need?" Swing asked.

They were passing a jewelry store, which had an illuminated clock over the entrance. She looked up at it. "It's

8:30 now. Let's give them until midnight, to be sure," she said. She smiled at Swing. "That will give us plenty of time to have *fun*." She pulled his arm closer against her hip.

This was a side of the Austrian agent that he had not seen before. He shrugged. "Whatever the sacrifice may be, we must perform our sworn duty. We owe it to the Emperor."

It was after midnight, long after midnight, when they staggered back into the lobby of the hotel. Swing could not remember the last time he had been so plastered. Actually, he could not remember very much of what he and his companion had done over the past few hours.

They claimed their room keys from the desk clerk and rode the creaking, old open-cage elevator to the fourth floor. They tottered together down the hall to Swing's room. Christina put a restraining hand on his shoulder, and knelt to examine the door handle. Suddenly, she did not look particularly drunk. In fact, as far as he could see, she appeared to be her usual, hyper-efficient self.

"This door has been forced," she whispered. She put an ear to the keyhole, and then pulled her silver automatic from a fold in her dress. "I better make sure they're gone." She said.

Her foot lashed into the door, flinging it open. Before it was completely open, she dove inside, performed a shoulder roll, and came up to one knee, gun in hand, ready to fire. The room was empty.

"It's all right, Ray," she said. "Come on in."

Swing's room looked as if some natural disaster had occurred there, a tornado, or perhaps an earthquake. The search had been conducted with brutal efficiency. Every drawer in the dresser had been pulled out and flung to the floor, the mattress had been cut open, then lifted from the bedframe and dropped to lean on the floor. The locks on his bags had been broken open, and the contents dumped out. The pockets of his suit jacket and pants had been turned out, and the lining of the jacket had been ripped away from the shell. Pages from his notebook lay scattered thickly on the floor. They stared at each other.

Swing broke into a happy grin. "That should be enough to satisfy them that I'm not carrying any secret papers, don't you think?" he asked. "I have to think we've seen the last of our two friends."

She smiled, and nodded. "I would be surprised if we see them again. Let's go see if they went into my room."

They went across the hall, where Christina paused briefly to examine the lock. "This one doesn't appear to have been opened," she said. She produced her key, unlocked the door, and they entered without taking any precautions. The room was exactly as she had left it.

"Apparently they believe I'm such a complete idiot that nobody would trust me with a burnt-out match, let alone state secrets," she commented. Her expression was compounded in equal parts of anger and amusement. "They didn't even bother to look in here."

"You kind of expected that, didn't you?" Swing asked. "I thought that was the whole point of assigning you, instead of a male agent. Which reminds me, where did you hide the papers?"

By way of an answer, Christina began to draw up her skirt. As Swing watched, the hem traveled north of her mid-thigh, then above her hip, until finally she held the garment just above her waist. Looped around the very tops of her thighs, taped in place just above the rolled tops of her silk stockings, was a pair of business envelopes.

"I thought they would be enough safe in here," she told

him. "They were a little uncomfortable when we were dancing, though." She continued to hold her skirt on high, out of politeness perhaps, as he was still inspecting her hiding place with wide eyes.

"Ah, yes… very safe… I imagine…" Swing agreed. He had seen a not few thighs in his day, but these were far and away the shapeliest in his experience. He licked his lips, which seemed to have suddenly gone dry. "Yes," he repeated absently, "very safe."

She sidled closer. "I suppose I don't need to hold on to them any longer," Christina said. "Why don't you take them back, Ray?" she suggested. She raised her left leg up against his hip, so that the taped envelope brushed his hand.

"Oh, yeah… I guess… I should," he agreed, gingerly surrounding the papers wrapped around her thigh with his hands.

He was not aware of it as it happened, but at some point he noticed that her arms were wrapped around his neck. "You know, Ray, you can't stay in your room tonight," she whispered in his ear. "They wrecked the room and destroyed your bed, and it's too late to get another room. The simplest thing would be for you to just stay here tonight."

"Here?" he asked nervously, his hands still wrapped around her leg.

Christina hooked the leg Swing was still holding around behind his back, trapping him in place, and at the same time pressed her body close against his, backing him up until he was half-sitting on the bed.

"Yes, Ray," she breathed. Her lips were less than an inch away from his, and closing the range. "Here with me." They were the last words either of them spoke for a very long time.

Paris Café in the 1920s

CHAPTER TEN
BERLIN, AUGUST 27, 1923

The Kaiser was in his very best mood. Indeed, he was in such excellent spirits that he was able to tolerate the report to the Cabinet by his Foreign Minister, Franz von Papen, a man who normally had the same effect on Wilhelm as fingernails scraped across a blackboard, without interruption. Papen was wrapping up his presentation with a summary of the Note from Emperor Charles handed in at his ministry earlier that day by the Austrian Ambassador.

"...he suggests that Germany is somehow implicit in the recent disturbances in Lublin, Cracow, Pinsk, Kiev and other cities where Your Majesty was forced to intervene to restore order, all without a shred of real proof, I must add..." Papen said, making a show of outrage. "There was also a not very carefully veiled accusation that Germany was involved in the formation of the new Magyar Republic, again a charge without the slightest basis in reality. The Emperor has therefore ordered his Ambassador home to protest to what he has the temerity to call 'intolerable German provocation and interference', and further states that normal diplomatic relations will not be restored until 'the illegal German incursion into the Empire territory is ended, and the areas under illegal occupation are returned to Imperial administration.' Both the language and content of this Note are intolerable, and go far beyond any acceptable diplomatic usage, Your Majesty. It is tantamount to a declaration of war."

The Foreign Minister's indignation was, of course, nothing more than a display of amateur dramatics. It was well known, at least among Wilhelm's chief Cabinet officers, that the disturbances in Poland and the Ukraine, and the revolution in Hungary had been secretly incited and underwritten by order of the Kaiser. The scheme had been cooked up by one Colonel Schleicher (whose name, appropriately enough, meant 'sneak' or 'intriguer' in German), a former aide of Groener's when the latter was the Chief of the General Staff, and taken up enthusiastically by the Kaiser. Since the agents used to carry out the scheme were being paid through the Foreign Ministry, as were the funds used to finance operation, Papen not only knew about the plan but was also, in fact, a participant in it.

Wilhelm smiled. "Yes, I suppose you are correct, but I think we must make allowances in this instance. My unfortunate Imperial cousin must be under a great strain at the moment, and I am quite certain that his words were written in the heat of the moment, as the result of a misunderstanding of my benign intentions. I have no doubt that, given time, Emperor Charles will eventually see that we are only acting to preserve the lives and property of his subjects, during this difficult period when he is unable to do so," he said blandly.

"Let us hope so, Your Majesty. It would be most unfortunate to lose our one real ally due to a *misunderstanding*," commented the Chancellor, Crown Prince Rupprecht, placing ironic stress on the final word. Wilhelm had sacked the Crown Prince's predecessor, Georg Michaelis, after the Martinique affair. Michaelis had been opposed to the plan adopted by the Kaiser, one that eventually led to a stinging diplomatic defeat for Germany, but the Kaiser had decided that the whole thing was somehow Michealis's fault. In any case, Wilhelm felt more comfortable when surrounded by military men and aristocrats, and Rupprecht qualified on both counts. He was the heir to the Bavarian throne, and he held the rank of Generaloberst. He had commanded the Sixth Army during the Great War.

Wilhelm's cheerful mood on this day was due to the success of his plans, which had been opposed by both the Crown Prince and Wilhelm Groener, the Minister of War. "Germany is strong, it is true, but not stronger than all the rest of the world together. The day may come when we will have need of a friend, and we will look around to find nothing but enemies." Groener said nothing, but looked at his colleague and nodded his heavy head to indicate his agreement.

"You are entitled to your opinions, gentlemen," the Kaiser answered, "but the final decisions on these matters must be mine, and you are obliged to accept them or else resign, something I think none of us wants. Now, was there anything else from the Foreign Ministry?" he asked, turning back to Papen.

"Yes, Your Majesty, there was one other item," responded the Foreign Minister. "We received a Note from Count Moric Esterhazy, the Foreign Minister of the Magyar Republic, requesting formal diplomatic recognition of the Karolyi government and an exchange of ambassadors between the two nations."

The Kaiser frowned. "Recognition?" he repeated. "That certainly seems premature, to say the least."

"Such course of action might easily be construed as an unfriendly act in Vienna," said the Chancellor, "and thus give rise to another misunderstanding."

"Quite true," Wilhelm said, ignoring the mildly caustic tone of the Crown Prince's remark. "On the other hand, if this new Magyar Republic is going to prove to be a stable and permanent feature of a new European alignment, it would be a mistake I think, to foreclose the possibility of making an arrangement with it. After all, there may come a time when we will have need of a friend, don't you agree, Prince Rupprecht?" he asked, fixing his gaze on the Chancellor. Hearing no reply, Wilhelm continued, "I suggest that we leave our relations with the Karolyi regime on an informal basis for now, without making any commitment, and wait to see how Vienna responds to the situation. If any of my ministers objects to this approach, I should like to hear his reasoning."

There was no objection, although it was clear that both the Chancellor and the Minister of War were suspicious of what lay behind this apparently innocuous decision. With that, the Kaiser rose and declared the Cabinet meeting concluded.

Groener and Prince Rupprecht dismissed their aides, and stayed on after everyone else had left the Cabinet chamber.

"I am certain that Wilhelm is already planning to recognize the new Hungarian state," the Minister of War said. "What do you think?"

"Absolutely," agreed the Crown Prince. "I have no doubt that he is already considering what he can squeeze out of the Hungarians in exchange. The Kaiser is shrewd, but not very intelligent, I fear. He is incapable of looking beyond the immediate moment and does not consider the long-term costs of these little victories."

Groener shook his head. "All he can see is new land added to his empire. He does not choose to think about how his own actions will bring about the very encirclement by enemies that he claims to fear. If Germany acts the bully, and is a constant menace to our neighbors, there can only be one result: we will eventually be surrounded by a ring of hostile powers. It would be no surprise if even the United States was now willing to join in an alliance against us. In the end, there will be another war, and I fear that *this* time, with the rest of the civilized world against us, we may not be as fortunate as we were in 1914."

The Chancellor rose. "If the Kaiser does grant recognition to the Magyar Republic, Wilhelm, I think I shall give him my resignation. I do not see that my continued service is doing Germany any good, and I grow weary of having my counsel mocked and ignored. I long to return to the Army or, failing that, take up the crown of Bavaria. Almost anything would be an improvement on this."

"Oh, you can't do that, my friend!" the Minister of War said earnestly. "That would be a disaster for Germany!"

"What makes you say so?" Rupprecht asked.

"If you go, he might make that ass Papen Chancellor, or even worse, someone like my old aide, that snake Schleicher," Groener said. "I think we might well be at war in eighteen months if you resigned."

"A year," corrected the Crown Prince. His mouth tightened, as if he were tasting something sour. "I suppose you are right. Perhaps if I continue to disagree with him, he will solve the problem for me and hand me the sack. "

"Let us hope not," the Minister of War said as they strode from the room together. "Things are bad enough as it is, but they are never so bad that they cannot get worse."

Berlin Stadtschloss

CHAPTER ELEVEN
VIENNA, AUGUST 28, 1923

Emperor Charles and his Prime Minister sat at a desk across in the Walnut Room of the Schoenbrunn Palace, each silently regarding the other, as if they were both waiting for the other to speak.

After what seemed to Sixtus like a sufficiently long period of silence, he cleared his throat and said, "It would seem that the military solution is not particularly appealing." He brushed his fingers over a leather binder with the Imperial coat of arms, a double-headed eagle with a multi-colored shield for a body, embossed on the cover, the written evaluation of the prospects for using the Army to end the Hungarian rebellion.

They had just been given an oral presentation by the Minister of War on this very subject. He did not present a very encouraging picture. According to the Ministry experts, approximately a quarter of the Army's formations would be more likely to fight *for* the new Magyar Republic than against it, if they were ordered to Budapest to suppress the revolt. In point of fact, several Generals had already declared that they intended to take service with the Karolyi government. It was further estimated that, as a result of conflicting loyalties, the combat efficiency of most of the remainder of the Army would be low to nil if they were sent out to kill fellow citizens of the Empire.

"Let us say that General von Webenau is being overly pessimistic, and it *is* possible to get the Army to fight the

Hungarians," the Emperor said, "what then? If we win, it will only mean God knows how many more killings, and afterwards what kind of state would we have, held together at gunpoint and poisoned with hate? I cannot see that the preservation of the Empire can possibly be worth the price in innocent lives that would have to be paid. As a Christian, I refuse to pay such a price."

"But Karl, the people of the Kingdom of Hungary are your responsibility," Sixtus protested. "If you abandon them, it means leaving the minorities in this... *Republic...*" he was barely able to force out the word, "...utterly at the mercy of those Magyarizing Hungarians, completely without a protector."

A troubled look crossed Karl's face. "I am aware of that, Sixtus. But I do not know what I can do to help them, short of starting a civil war. And given the hatreds that would be unleashed in such a conflict, I think it would make the American Civil War look like..." he paused, searching for an appropriate comparison.

"Like a tea party on the vicar's lawn," Sixtus finished. "No, I agree. A civil war is unthinkable. But then what will we do?"

"The truth is that we have very little choice under the circumstances," the Emperor said. "We must accept the inevitable. I shall announce that the Compromise of 1867 has been terminated and is null and void, and let Hungary go its own way."

"There must be something else we can try short of that," his brother-in-law protested. "Could we not at least attempt to negotiate a new Compromise that would leave some connection between us? Hungary has been ruled by your family for almost four hundred years. Surely there is no harm in making an effort to preserve something from the wreck."

Karl shook his head. "I have more than five hundred excellent reasons for believing that there is no hope in negotiations at this point," he said, referring to the number of the dead from the massacre in Budapest. "I think it is best to do what needs to be done in a peaceful fashion and generous spirit. Only this can begin to alleviate some of the bitterness."

Sixtus said nothing, but his expression indicated that he still was not wholly convinced by the Emperor's arguments.

"It is not as if this was totally unexpected, after all," Karl continued. "I for one never thought that the creation of 1867 would last forever. There is little doubt in my mind that the great majority of Hungarians have wanted to part ways with Austria at least as long ago as 1848..." when a Hungarian independence movement was bloodily suppressed by a combination of Austrian and Russian troops "...and nothing has happened since then to make the union more popular in Budapest."

"True enough," Sixtus agreed reluctantly.

"There is a bright side, if you care to look for it," Karl continued. "The Hungarians have opposed my programs for political reform and economic development at every turn, and now we will be able to proceed without the dead hand of what is, after all, a comparatively backward, rural nation. I suspect that, in the not very long run, the new Magyar Republic will prove to be so dependent on Austria economically that they will be subject to us for all practical purposes and independent in name only."

"There is that," the Prince said. He brightened. "And of course, without you to mitigate their excesses, when they start to get rough with the non-Magyars, their ethnic minorities will scream bloody murder, and they will soon find themselves on the brink of war with Romania and Russia, whereas for us, those particular headaches will be things of the past."

"I cannot take any pleasure in the prospect of war, no matter which parties are involved," Karl said reprovingly. "However, leaving aside your enthusiasm for your prediction, I must agree. I think we have discussed the matter sufficiently, and I hope that if you are still incompletely persuaded, you will still put aside your reservations and help me. Will you prepare a draft speech granting Hungarian independence for my consideration, Sixtus? I will work on my own version, and we can compare notes tomorrow."

"Yes, of course I will, Your Majesty," Sixtus said, rising. "The truth is that the Hungarians do not deserve to be ruled by such a decent human being. They are barbarians."

"Whether they deserve me or I them is in any case irrelevant," the Emperor said. "In a few days, they won't have King Charles the Fourth to kick around any more."

Chartwell House, Westerham, Kent

CHAPTER TWELVE
WESTERHAM, ENGLAND,
SEPTEMBER 1, 1923

As the Prime Minister absolutely refused to conduct business in London over the weekend, the meeting with Swing was moved to Chartwell, the P.M.'s newly acquired country estate in Kent. Churchill insisted that the reporter and his photographer stay on as his guests from Friday to Sunday.

"I have a great many things to discuss, Mr. Swing, and I will not be rushed through them. We shall have all of the weekend to cover them," the Prime Minister said.

It was early Saturday afternoon before they even began to talk. Swing, Churchill and Sir Edward Grey, the Foreign Secretary, had just finished a long lunch consisting of several courses of solid English food, including a bland, unsauced whiting, a Yorkshire pudding and a large and (to Swing's mind) overcooked roast beef, and were now settled into leather wing chairs in the drawing room which was lit by 18th century crystal chandeliers and had a fine view of the Kentish countryside. Christina had been taken on a tour of the grounds by the P.M.'s wife, Clementine.

The Prime Minister had a brandy close at hand on a side table. He took a sip, and regarded the American through a cloud of cigar smoke. "I have read the draft treaty you have brought from us from Vienna," he said. "If his proposal is to be taken at face value, it would appear that Emperor Charles wishes to make this Grand Alliance..." (this name for the proposed treaty was Churchill's own coining, and it was a moment before Swing realized what he was talking about) "...open to any nation who cares to join it. May I take this to mean that you have already discussed it with Signore Giolotti , and Monsieurs Theunis..." (the heads of the Italian and Belgian governments) "... and Herriot, and that you further plan to seek allies in the Hague, Copenhagen, Stockholm and St. Petersburg? If he hoped to keep his plans *sub rosa*, I should think this would be a chancy procedure, at best." The latter four cities would follow Swing's stop in England.

Swing had the strong impression that this question was not intended seriously, but he chose to treat it as if it was. "Well no, sir," Swing said. "It was the Emperor's idea that the treaty proposal be made only here, to France and the United States, to begin with. Only after the..." he paused for a moment, and then decided to adopt the Prime Minister's terminology "...Grand Alliance was a going concern, would other nations be invited."

"Prudent," commented the Foreign Secretary, blowing out a cloud of cigarette smoke. "Aside from the issue of security, I am uncertain to what degree the treaty Powers would be strengthened by the addition of Belgium, Denmark, the Netherlands and other smaller states, particularly if it entails an automatic commitment to war in the event they are threatened by Germany."

"Indeed," agreed Churchill. "This was almost the first thought that occurred to me as I perused the proposal. It is possible to imagine the French being willing to make such a commitment, if by doing so they were able to gain allies such as Austria and the United States. It is conceivable, at least since the recent crisis in the Western Hemisphere..." by which he meant the Martinique Affair "...to foresee the Commons agreeing to make this country part of such a combination, but I do not see any way that the great Republic on the far side of the Atlantic would be ready to do so, at least not in the immediate future, as you should understand as well as anyone, Mr. Swing. We are presently engaged in talks with the Americans, and there is an excellent prospect for the signing of a naval treaty between us in the near future..." for confirmation he turned to Gray, who nodded, then continued, "...largely thanks to Kaiser Wilhelm, but is your nation, so recently emerged from isolation, prepared to enter a European war of behalf of Denmark or Holland? I rather think not."

Swing did not attempt to gainsay Churchill's shrewd observation. Indeed, he thought it would be difficult to even get the Americans to sit down at the conference table to just to discuss joining such an alliance system. "Those are the sorts of matters that can be straightened out at the conference. The details can be worked out later. The important thing is to begin, if it is not too late already," Swing said.

"Ah, there I think you have put your finger on the salient point," Churchill said. "Perhaps our position in the world would not today be so perilous had we stood by France and Russia in their hour of need in 1914. Now Germany is stronger, far stronger I fear, than she was a decade ago, and the other powers of Central and Eastern Europe, weaker. Even with the adherence of the United States to an alliance with ourselves, France, and Austria, the outcome of a war with Germany would be far from certain, particularly in view of Austria's current difficulties. But still, *late* is better far than *never*, and it is something to start, to make a stand, before first Europe, then all the world, is submerged beneath the gray, Teutonic tide. There have been far too many wars in the long, lamentable catalogue of human cruelty, and far too many innocents have been made to pay in blood for decisions in which they had no say. No sane man would wish for war, but there are some things which are worse still, Mr. Swing, and at certain times in history we must be prepared to fight to preserve our honor and our liberty."

"I have seen modern warfare firsthand, Mr. Churchill, I have reported on it..." Swing began.

"And, as one who made his debut in public life as a war correspondent, done so exceedingly well, may I say," Churchill interposed.

"Thank you, sir," Swing acknowledged the compliment, then continued, "...and although I could not phrase it as eloquently as you, I agree with every word you said. Germany must be stopped soon, or it will be too late to stop her at all. This is exactly why I agreed to take on this mission for the Emperor, and why I will do everything in my power to persuade President Lowden to send the Secretary of State or another U.S. representative with plenipotentiary powers to the treaty conference when I return to America."

"Then, let us hope that your persuasive powers are at a maximum when you meet the President," Churchill said, "as I suspect that you will be undertaking a formidable assignment. You may be assured that, at least as far as His Majesty's Government is concerned, you have accomplished the Emperor's purpose: we shall certainly be in attendance at the treaty conference in October. Now let us turn to other matters. As you have so recently met with the Emperor, I should like to hear how you believe he will deal with the Hungarian crisis..."

The talk continued through dinner, and until well after midnight.

CHAPTER THIRTEEN
BUDAPEST, SEPTEMBER 3, 1923

Mihaly Karolyi, Provisional President of the freshly minted Magyar Republic (*President!* He could still scarcely believe it) gaveled the cabinet meeting to order. The first topic was a proposal from Germany, which was presented by the Foreign Minister, Count Esterhazy.

After reading the Note aloud to the assembled Cabinet, he summarized it, presumably for those members of the government who were unfamiliar with the language of diplomacy: "...in short, Germany will agree to extend diplomatic recognition to this Government, in return for our agreement to recognize German rights in certain disputed regions of Poland, Ruthenia and Ukraine..."

"The territory the Kaiser snatched from the Empire, you mean," interrupted Minister of War, Horthy. "He wants us to approve his thefts, with diplomatic recognition as the bribe for our acquiescence, is that about right?" the blunt-spoken former naval officer inquired acidly.

Count Esterhazy did not care for Horthy, and he did not much care who knew it. He looked down his long nose at his colleague, his expression suggesting that he had detected an offensive odor. "I would consider that an exceedingly crude interpretation of the Note, even by your standards," he began. "In diplomatic usage..."

Karolyi rose to his feet, and hurriedly interrupted, "Thank you, Your Excellency." The two men had tangled before, and he thought it prudent to intervene before another violent argument disrupted the business of the government again. It was clear that the two men would not be able to serve together in the same government, and he was preparing to allow Count Esterhazy to pursue other career opportunities. "I believe we all have an adequate understanding of the nature of the German offer. I should like to hear the other Ministers thoughts on it."

The debate that followed was desultory. The Cabinet members, with the exception of Horthy, had been chosen for their political connections rather than their ability, as Karolyi believed that the first requirement for the new republic's survival was to make the political base of the government as broad as possible. The resulting cabinet however, suffered from a dearth of talent. On the roster of nonentities that constituted the cabinet of the Magyar Republic, only the former naval officer, Horthy, had displayed any sign of original thought, energy or ability to govern. The majority of the Ministers were clearly still confused and frightened by the sudden change in Hungary's status, and were unable or unwilling to adjust their thinking to the present. As soon as the country was on a firm footing, Karolyi was determined to replace them all (with the exception of the Minister of War) with men of real ability.

Other than Horthy, none of the cabinet members expressed a firm opinion on the question before them, asked an intelligent question, or made any worthwhile comment. They were waiting hear the President's stance so that they could go on record as agreeing with the boss, who also happened to be the most popular figure in Hungarian politics since the beloved leader of the 1848 revolution, Lajos Kossuth.

Horthy, by contrast, was not afraid to express his view,

which was that the Kaiser's offer should be rejected. "It is not merely a craven act on our part, but it will prove to be the first step in poisoning our relations with Austria forever, and so leave us dependent on Germany. We need to keep a strong economic connection with the Empire. Please remember that compared with Austria, we are a poor and backward nation. It will be far easier for Vienna to look elsewhere for raw materials and markets for their manufactures than for us to do so. Then again, what if the Kaiser decides to claim a few choice bits of *our* territory? Who will sympathize with Hungary when, I say *when* not *if*, that happens? The Emperor Charles has already recognized our status as an independent state; what do we need with German approval? I say we tell Kaiser Wilhelm that we don't give a pin whether he recognizes us or not. We should show strength; the Germans have no respect for weakness."

Karolyi thought that there was a great deal to be said for the Minister of War's arguments, but in the end he felt that the immediate need to get the new nation established outweighed the risks outlined by Horthy, which, although they were very real, were prospective only, and the demands of the present situation took precedence. He therefore told the Cabinet his view, and asked for a vote. There was only a single negative vote, and Karolyi instructed Count Esterhazy to prepare the response to Germany.

The meeting continued for another hour before Karolyi called it a day. The Ministers filed out, leaving the room to the President and Horthy, whom the former had asked to remain behind.

"I wanted to know if you took care of that little matter I asked you to handle for me," Karolyi said.

"You mean that Wolf fellow?" Horthy asked. "All done.

I told the German government that he had been a great help to us and should be rewarded, but that we wanted him ordered home, and they agreed. He is…" he looked up at a wall clock, "…already on a train to Berlin."

"Good," Karolyi said. He grimaced. "I did not like for the man; he made me very uncomfortable for some reason."

"He did seem a bit… intense," Horthy agreed. "Incidentally, I found out a little about his background, if you're interested."

"Oh?"

"He was born in a little town in Upper Austria, moved to Germany and volunteered for service with the Bavarians in the war," Horthy said. "He was a war hero, wounded in combat, and decorated, twice I think."

"Interesting," Karolyi said. "Well, thank you, Miklos. I'm just glad that I won't have to see him again."

Horthy rose and began to leave the room. As he was opening the door, Karolyi asked casually, "Did you ever find out what his real name was? I assume it was not Wolf?"

"Yes," Horthy said, pausing with his hand on the doorknob, "it was something like… Hiller… no, *Hit*ler," he corrected himself. "Adolf Hitler."

CHAPTER FOURTEEN
WASHINGTON, D.C.,
SEPTEMBER 12, 1923

The meeting concluded, Ray Swing stood and shook hands with President Lowden. "Thank for taking the time to meet me, Mr. President," he said. He then shook hands with and thanked Secretary of State Wood and the President's personal secretary Joseph McCormick, and left the Oval Office. After the door closed behind him, the three men resumed their seats around the President's desk.

"Well, General," the President asked Wood, "what is your evaluation of the Austrian treaty proposal?"

"I think I would like to examine the language of the draft treaty before making any definite commitments…" he began cautiously.

"I am not asking for you for anything in writing, nor a formal analysis of any kind," Lowden cut in. "I just want your impressions based on one reading of the treaty and the Emperor's letter. Should the United States send a representative to this conference, and would it be in our national interest to be a party to such a treaty?"

"If you asked me that question six months ago, I would have said 'no' and 'no'," the Secretary of State answered. "It is absolutely contrary to the tradition of American foreign policy to make this type of treaty arrangement with any European state, and risk being dragged into one of their wars. But now…" He paused.

"Yes?" Lowden prompted. "Now, what? You have a different opinion, perhaps?"

"Yes, I think I do," Wood replied. He hesitated, took a deep breath, and said, "Since our little tango with the Germans this spring, I have become more and more in agreement with Swing and the internationalists. Germany is a menace, and I do not believe that the ocean constitutes the safeguard of our security that it once did. Nor do I think that we are so strong that we can afford to ignore what happens in the rest of the world. I not only believe that we should attend the Vienna conference, but, assuming the final treaty did not call upon us to make unacceptable commitments, I would recommend we sign it, possibly as an Associated Power or some such, with specifically delineated and limited military obligations, perhaps."

"I don't doubt that your old boss, were he here, would have agreed with you," Lowden said, "but then the prospect of war didn't scare T.R., did it?"

"No sir," Wood answered. "But then not very much of anything *did* scare him. I believe you could have held a loaded gun to his face and it would not have bothered him. In any event, you have my view."

"For which I am grateful, as always," Lowden said.

"If you do not have anything else for me, Mr. President, please excuse me. I should return to my office," Wood said, as he stood up.

"Yes, of course," the President said. "We will speak about this further tomorrow."

After the Secretary of State departed, Lowden turned to McCormick. "Well, Joseph, I could not help but notice that you did not have much to say. I'll wager you were listening pretty carefully, though."

"You'd win that bet," McCormick said.

"So, would you care to share your thoughts on the Austrian treaty with me?" Lowden asked.

"If you want me to think of it as foreign policy," he answered, "I'll pass. What do I know about foreign policy? But if you want my take on the political implications...?"

"Yes, Joseph, I would," Lowden said patiently. "Must I remind you that you are my chief political advisor?"

"Boss, before the Martinique crisis, I would have said that even hinting that you were considering a treaty like this one would be political suicide," McCormick said. "But things have changed. I think now you might have the votes in the Senate for approval of it, in some form, at least. The war scare made an impression on the public and the Senators know it. People are really aware of the threat of Germany now, and they may just be ready for something like this. The naval treaty with the British will be a good test of the support you can expect for the Austrian proposal. I anticipate it to get at least 85 votes in the Senate. The only ones you won't get are the real hard-shell Midwestern isolationists."

"Meaning Bob Lafollette and company, I presume," Lowden said.

"His influence is at a low ebb right now," McCormick said. "For the time being at least, the isolationists are isolated. If you were to explain the purpose of the treaty to the country, say on a series of radio addresses, I think you'd find the country is ready to listen, and to follow you."

"Are they ready to follow me if I tell them I want to build up a big army and expand the Navy in peacetime? And if the treaty draws us into a war in Europe, will they still follow me?" Lowden asked.

McCormick nodded. "I think they just might, boss. I

really do."

"So it is not a matter whether we *can* do it, but merely of whether we *should*," Lowden said. "We are at a fork in the road of history, Joseph, and the wrong decision may lead this nation down into the abyss. It seems that the power to choose has, for some reason, been given into my hands."

"I've said it before, boss, and I'll say it again," McCormick said. "I wouldn't want to trade places with you. But these are the kinds of decisions that come with the job. If it helps any, you know that whatever you decide, I'm behind you all the way."

The President rose, and clapped his hand on his secretary's shoulder. "It is a great comfort to me, Joseph. Thank you."

McCormick clapped his hat on his head, said, "Good night, boss," and left. After the door closed behind him, Lowden told his secretary to hold all his calls. He leaned back in his chair, put his feet up on his desk, and sat for a long time in silence, gazing out his office window at the capital bathing in the moonlight.

A few blocks away, Ray Swing was at that moment also gazing at the city of Washington under the full moon through the window of his hotel room. Unlike the President, however, he was not alone.

"What are you thinking about, Ray?" a warm contralto voice asked.

He rolled over in the bed to face his companion. "Oh, nothing in particular, Christina," he answered. "I'm just wondering whether the whole trip was just a waste of time, or if there really will be a Grand Alliance."

"So?" The Austrian agent moved closer, pressing her body against him. Her lips were slightly parted, and he felt the heat of her breath on his cheek. "What do you think will happen?"

"Well, to tell you the truth, it's a little hard to concentrate at this exact second," he answered. He slid his arms around her and they kissed, and then proceeded on to other things.

Later, they lay side-by-side on top of the sheets, their bodies gleaming with sweat. "I don't suppose you can arrange to stay on for a few more days in the States," Swing said.

She shook her head. "I wish I could, Ray, but my orders are to return to Vienna immediately. They need every trained agent right away."

"That's understandable," he said. "The break-up of the Empire is bound to be a huge mess, even when everyone involved has the best intentions." The newspapers had been filled with stories of protest marches, riots, mass arrests and shootings in the Romanian, Czech, Slovak and Polish areas of the Magyar Republic, and less serious disorders in the Austrian Empire. In addition, Russia, Romania, and Bulgaria were making threatening noises, and the Germans seemed ready to take advantage of any civil unrest by occupying more of their neighbor's property. All of Central and Eastern Europe was in chaos, and it was far from clear whether the shrunken Austrian Empire or its newly independent Hungarian offspring would survive what was coming.

"This won't be our last night together, Ray." Christina said reassuringly. "I'll see you the next time you come to Europe on assignment."

"That's right, of course you will," Swing agreed. "Now that I think about it, the *Inquirer* will probably send me over to Vienna to cover the treaty conference next month. That's only a few weeks from now."

She smiled, leaned over, and kissed him again. "It's a date."

Washington in moonlight

CHAPTER FIFTEEN
VIENNA, OCTOBER 11, 1923

In fact, it proved impossible for Swing to find Christina. All his inquiries at the Ministry of the Interior led nowhere. The officials he spoke to refused to pass on any message from him to her. They would not acknowledge that such a person as Christina Dietrichstein was employed by the Austrian government, or that she even existed. His attempts to use his personal connections with the Emperor and Prince Parma-Bourbon were no more successful. He was not even able to schedule a meeting with either man until, after his fifth try, Sixtus agreed to see him privately for a few minutes.

"I must apologize for our apparent lack of gratitude for what you did for us, Ray," the Prince said. They were seated in Sixtus' study adjoining his private office in the Hofburg Palace, the winter seat of the Hapsburg dynasty. "You must believe me when I tell you that we recognize the great debt you are owed. Emperor Karl would like to confer the Order of Leopold on you for your work in bringing about the Grand Alliance conference, as a partial payment, but we are rather busy right now."

"I know that, and I didn't want to bother you at such a critical time, but I must ask a personal favor," Swing said. He recounted his search for Christina, and its singular lack of success. "Since you are the Minister of the Interior, not to mention the Prime Minister, I figured you could help me."

When he finished, Sixtus looked at him gravely. "I would

very much like to help you, my friend, but you must understand that Agent Dietrichstien is on an official mission for the Ministry at this time. She is for all practical purposes a soldier, one who is on active duty. I could not interfere with the performance of her duty for personal reasons, not even for you."

Swing's shoulders slumped. "I understand. Of course you are right. I'm sorry to have wasted your time."

"It is never a waste of time to see old friends again," the Prince said. "The Emperor and I will have you in for dinner and a long talk very soon, I promise. And do not despair of seeing your friend again. She may turn up when you least expect her."

Thereafter, Swing put Christina out of his thoughts and concentrated on his assignment interviewing diplomatic representatives of the participating nations, talking to experts and covering developments in the treaty negotiations. On the first day he had been pleased to run into his old friend Joe Stilwell, who had been selected as the military attaché to the American delegation. Stilwell had been promoted since the last time he and Swing had met, and was now sporting the silver leaves of a Lieutenant Colonel on his shoulders. The two men spent the first evening after the close of the conference catching up on their activities over the past two years, the last time they had met.

"I had just managed to wangle a transfer to a line command when I was called back to Washington and informed that my services would be required here," Stilwell explained. "It seems that I am now *the* official expert on the weapons, tactics and general capabilities of the German Army, and the conference just wouldn't be the same without me," he said.

"On the other hand, I imagine your expertise in that

particular subject has helped your career along," Swing guessed.

"Maybe," Stilwell admitted, "but if it also means that I'm going to be permanently assigned to the paper-shuffling brigade, I'd rather still be a Captain in command of soldiers, even if it was only a company."

Stilwell was particularly entertained by the reporter's account of how he and Christina had shaken off the two foreign agents who were shadowing him. "That's a peach!" he said, laughing. "Peachy" or "a peach" was Stilwell's ultimate term of praise. "You outsmarted them by pretending to be stupider than they were. That Austrian agent sounds like quite a gal," he added. "I'd like to meet her. Is she in Vienna now?"

"I don't know," Swing said, and immediately changed the subject

On the eighth day of the conference the delegates were given the morning off. Swing and Stilwell sat together at an outdoor café on the *Ringstrasse* in the center of town, munching rich Viennese pastries and sipping hot chocolate, reading the newspapers and talking over the current European political picture.

"It looks like the Hungarians may be in over their heads," Stilwell said, as he rapidly read through an article in the *Daily Telegraph*. "The Czechs and Slovaks left inside the old borders of the Kingdom of Hungary want to join the Austrian Empire, the Romanians in Transylvania want to join the Kingdom of Romania, and the Croats are calling for their own independent state. The Romanians have mobilized their army, and the Hungarian Army, such as it is, has its hands full already putting out all the fires."

"Chickens coming home to roost," Swing said. "Their ethnic policies made a lot of internal enemies for the

Hungarians, and now they're paying the price. How are they responding in Budapest?"

"It looks like they're pushing the panic button," Stilwell answered. "Karolyi has canned the entire Cabinet with the exception of the Minister of War, and will be forming a new government today."

"Meanwhile, Austria seems to have weathered the storm," Swing said. He was reading a day-old edition of the *Paris Herald*. "The new Czech-Slovak Parliament passed a resolution confirming its loyalty to the Empire, and everything seems to be calm elsewhere. Makes an interesting contrast with the Magyar Republic, don't you think?"

Before Stilwell could respond, a woman who had appeared out of nowhere said, "Very interesting, I agree. Hi, Ray. Who's your friend?" Without waiting for an answer, she pulled up a chair and sat down. She was tall, had short, black hair, and was, to Swing, as desirable as ever.

"Christina!" Swing gasped. "Prince Sixtus told me you were on an assignment..."

"I was," she interrupted, smiling. "Since your companion has forgotten his manners, I'll introduce myself. My name is Christina Dietrichstien, at one time photographer for the famous reporter, Ray Swing."

Stilwell laughed. "You know, I was going to guess that." He rose and offered his hand. "Nice meeting you, Miss Diedrichtstien." He glanced at Swing, who was staring at the Austrian girl as if he was having a vision. "It looks as if you two have some catching up to do, and I have some papers to shuffle, so I'll be running along. See you later, Ray." With that, he picked up his hat from the table, settled it on his head and departed.

Christina reached over the table to take Swing's hand in

hers. "It's so good to see you again, Ray."

He squeezed her hand. "I didn't think I was going to see you again. I had just about given up on it."

"Well, I was on a mission for the Bureau," she said. "And now I have a new assignment, starting today."

"Oh," Swing tried unsuccessfully to hide his disappointment. "Didn't they give you any time off at all between jobs, not even a day?"

"No, I was ordered to start immediately," she answered in a surprisingly cheerful tone. "It is considered a very high-priority assignment."

Swing wondered how she could announce such bad news so light-heartedly. "Oh, hell," he said. "What is the assignment, anyway?" he asked dully, staring down at the table.

"Prince Sixtus is worried about the safety of a visiting American journalist, and I was assigned to protect him," Christina answered. She grinned as he looked up at her, his expression brightening. "I have been designated as your bodyguard until you return to the U.S. I hope that is acceptable."

Swing's smile was so wide that it was almost painful. "I guess that would be all right," he said.

Imperial Coat of Arms of the Empire of Austria by Sodacan
based on a work by Hugo Gerhard Ströhl (1851–1919)

CHAPTER SIXTEEN

From the editorial page of the *Philadelphia Inquirer*,
November 15, 1923
by Raymond Swing, Foreign Affairs Editor

...The ratification of the Trans-Atlantic Treaty by the United States, in tandem with the recently adopted Anglo-American Hemispheric Naval Agreement, marks the beginning of a new era in American foreign policy. For the first time in its history, this nation has undertaken treaty obligations in conjunction with foreign powers. It is sobering to think that these obligations may someday lead us into a foreign war, and such a risk is not to be taken lightly.

But, in the view of this reporter, it was the right thing to do. The new Trans-Atlantic Treaty Organization of which the United States is now a member, rather than increasing the risk of war, represents the best chance to avoid it. The member states are pledged to join together to defend each other against any aggressor nation. TATO will provide security for all, by presenting any aggressor with a united front of Great Powers, which no single nation, no matter how strong, can hope to defeat. As Mr. Churchill, the Prime Minister of Great Britain so aptly put it, "There are times when the surest way to prevent war is to be prepared for it."

We have, as a nation, given up something precious by taking on new responsibilities outside of our traditions. No longer will America have the freedom to stand apart from the troubles of the Old World. But the ocean barriers that once protected this Republic now constitute potential highways for invasion. The world has become a smaller place than the one in which our Founding Fathers lived, and a more dangerous one, and we can no longer safely ignore events on the other side of the Atlantic, nor pretend that they cannot affect us. Let us pray that the military conventions of the new treaty are never invoked, and that we are not drawn into a new great war. But if such a war does come, it is worth considering that our participation will not merely be in the interests of the United States, but will be in the defense of freedom from tyranny for all the world.

AFTERWORD

The Austro-Hungarian Empire was in 1914 the second-largest country in Europe (after the Russian Empire), and one of the world's Great Powers. It does not nowadays claim a very prominent role in history, at least as the subject is taught in American schools. About all that anyone remembers about it is that the assassination of the Imperial heir, Archduke Franz Ferdinand, on June 28, 1914, was in some way the proximate cause of the First World War. The plot of the story is driven to a large degree by the history and politics of this long-vanished nation, and I have attempted to provide sufficient historical information in the body of the story to explain the motives and actions of the characters portrayed therein. But, it seemed to me that a brief essay on the history and politics of the Dual Monarchy might provide readers with a useful context for the fictitious events depicted in the preceding story.

The Austro-Hungarian Empire, which was erased from the map after World War One, was a bizarre political contraption, in part an antique relict from the Holy Roman Empire, in part a by-product of defeat by Bismarck's Prussia in 1866. Austria had been the seat of the Central European branch of the Hapsburgs since the 13th Century. In 1526 the dynasty inherited the Crown of St. Stephen. Thereafter, the two nations were for many years linked only by the person of the common ruler, who was at once the Emperor of Austria and the King of Hungary. Hungary retained many of the elements of sovereignty, with its own parliament (the Diet), government and budget, but it lacked two essential attributes of an independent nation: it lacked both its own currency and an army. In addition, the Imperial bureaucracy that administered the entire Dual Monarchy was controlled by Vienna. By the middle of the 19th Century, Hungary was slowly losing its quasi-autonomous status within the Empire.

Thus, Hungary was ripe for an independence movement in 1848, when a wave of liberal, nationalist revolutions threatened to overthrow monarchical governments from France to Poland, and from Denmark to Italy. In Hungary, a revolution led by lawyer and politician Lajos Kossuth initially succeeded in driving out the Hapsburg government, but the independent nation he created was soon crushed by an army of 300,000 Russians under Czar Nicholas I. Afterwards, the Hungarian Diet and government were suspended, and the Kingdom was governed exclusively from Vienna. Kossuth became a popular hero and symbol of Hungarian national aspirations.

In 1866, Austria and its allies were crushed by Prussia in the Seven Weeks War. The costs of this war combined with those stemming from a defeat at the hands of France and Sardinia in 1859, had brought the Empire to the brink of collapse, with an enormous state debt and a growing fiscal crisis. In order to stave off complete dissolution of the Empire, the government of Emperor Franz Joseph was forced to offer the Hungarians the Compromise of 1867, in return for Hungary's agreement to take on a share of the Imperial debt, and to leave foreign policy in the hands of Austria. Under the terms of this agreement, Hungary's independent legislature, government and separate budget were restored, and Budapest was granted what amounted to a monopoly of political power within the borders of the Transleithania (i.e. the Kingdom of

Hungary).

This latter provision aggravated an internal problem for which the Dual Monarchy never found a solution, the problem of the ethnic minorities. There were more than ten major languages spoken within the Empire (major being defined as more than 700,000 speakers), including German, Hungarian, Czech, Polish and Serbo-Croatian. While some of these groups enjoyed comparatively favored status within the Empire (such as the Poles in the Austrian half and the Croats in the Hungarian), none had been granted what amounted to an autonomous state within the Empire, except for the Hungarians. Particularly displeased with the new arrangement were roughly 6 million Czechs, 3 million Romanians and the nearly 2 million Slovaks in the newly autonomous Kingdom of Hungary, who had virtually no say in how they were governed.

After 1867, Hungary and Austria began to part ways on the handling of the ethnic minorities, which aggravated the internal stresses that were pulling the Empire apart. In Austria the heir, Franz Ferdinand, came to believe that the nation could not survive unless its Slavic subjects were given a fair share of political power within the Empire. Various plans to dismantle the German monopoly of power in Austria and replace it with a federal system under which the minorities would have a share of the government began to gain influential adherents, such as Franz Ferdinand's nephew, Charles. The Christian Socialist Party platform of 1905 proposed to reform the Cisleithania by creating a federation consisting of 15 ethnic nation-states under the Imperial umbrella. ("The Dismantling of Historic Hungary: The Peace Treaty of Trianon, 1920" by Ignác Romsics, p.11.)

Unfortunately for the proponents of these schemes, by the time Charles ascended the throne in 1916 it was too late to do anything to implement them. The war had virtually destroyed the Empire. All that remained was a shell operated by Germany in order to keep the Austrian army fighting.

The Hungarians demonstrated their favored approach to the nationalities problem even before the Revolution of 1848, with a series of laws requiring the exclusive use of the Magyar in public life. It was required for admission to the bar (1831); made the official language of laws passed by the Diet (1838); the exclusive language for all government administration (1843); mandatory in secondary education (1844); and a test for voters (1848). This last was a product of Kossuth's "liberal" regime. After 1867, the suppression of the minorities within Hungary, now called "Magyarization", resumed. For the Magyar-speaking minority (roughly 48% of the population) this was the one policy that virtually all Hungarian political parties could agree upon. The pressure from the dissatisfied minorities continued to build through 1914, and it played a major part in the final dissolution of the Empire in 1918.

In addition to these internal problems, the Empire was beset by external foes. To the northeast, there loomed the menace of the Russians who, under the doctrine of Pan-Slavism, claimed the role of protectors of their ethnic kin, particularly those living within Austria-Hungary. In furtherance of this policy, Russia had a bi-lateral treaty with Serbia, under which the Czar was obligated to come to the aid of latter country if she was attacked by Austria-Hungary. It was this connection that led directly to the outbreak of the First World War, after the assassination of Archduke Franz Ferdinand by Serb nationalists.

Then there was the relatively new independent Kingdom of Romania (1878), on the eastern border of Hungary. Directly adjacent to Romania was Transylvania, legendary home of vampires and part of the Hungary since 1690. The majority of the province were ethnic Romanians, and after 1867, their desire to leave the Empire and join Romania grew steadily, as did the possibility of war.

In the south, the Kingdom of Serbia exerted a magnetic attraction on millions of South Slavs inside the Empire. The fear that Franz Ferdinand's plan to extend political rights to their fellows, and thus quell their desire to leave the Empire, motivated the men who plotted the assassination in Sarajevo which touched off the World War.

The southwest bordered on the Kingdom of Italy. Italy claimed that the Trentino, Trieste, South Tyrol, Istria and Gorzia were all rightfully part of Italy. Since Italy and the Empire were partners in the Triple Alliance of 1882 (Germany was the third member), the two nations were theoretically allies. On the other hand, Italy had never dropped its claims to the afore-mentioned Imperial territories, and thus constituted yet another potential threat to the Dual Monarchy. This threat became a reality when, in 1915, Italy joined the Entente and declared war on Austria.

It was not surprising, in view of all of the above, that four years of total war caused the ramshackle structure to finally collapse in 1918. In retrospect, it is more surprising that the Empire was able to endure for as long as it did.

For information on the politics and policies of the Empire, and the various approaches to the minorities issue, including federalism and Magyarism, "The Dismantling of Historic Hungary: The Peace Treaty of Trianon, 1920" by Ignác Romsics; *translated by* Mario D. Fenyo, in *The International History Review* Vol. 26, No. 1 (Mar., 2004) proved to be indispensable.

Extremely helpful as source for the economic

relationships between Germany, Austria and Hungary in the decade following the War was *The Danube Basin and the German Economic Sphere* by Antonin Basch, (New York, 1943).

I am indebted to **Steven Sowards for his lucid and informative lecture** "Nationalism in Hungary, 1848-1867" (Michigan State University, April 23, 2004), one of his *Twenty-Five Lectures in Balkan History*, (http://staff.lib.msu.edu/sowards/balkan/lect07.htm).

Some readers may find the Emperor Karl's choice of an American reporter to be his diplomatic courier unlikely, but in fact, Raymond Swing was asked by the Chancellor of Germany to carry a confidential message to the British Foreign Minister, Sir Edward Grey, during the First World War. (http://www.spartacus.schoolnet.co.uk/2WWswingR.htm)

For background on Churchill and Chartwell, I relied on William Manchester's superb biography, *The Last Lion: Alone 1932-1940* (Boston, Toronto, London, 1988). I recommend this book and the first volume, *Visions of Glory, 1874-1932* to anyone who is interested in the life of this towering figure.

I was unable to find any biographical information concerning the Managing Editor of the *Philadelphia Inquirer*, John T. Curtis (who was apparently not related to the famous Curtis family, publishers of the *Saturday Evening Post* and later the *Inquirer*), beyond a few cryptic references, as in the March 6, 1930 *Scranton Republican* cited below.

(http://www.newspapers.com/newspage/49784700/)

For details of the interior of the Schonbrunn see (http://www.schoenbrunn.at/en.html)

Following are short biographical sketches of the principal historical characters in order of their appearances in the story. (Those whose biographical material follows the first story are so noted).

Prince Sixtus of Bourbon-Parma by Hoffotograf - Wikipedia-de

Prince Sixtus of Bourbon-Parma (1886-1934) was the son of Robert, Duke of Parma, and brother-in-law of Emperor Charles I of Austria-Hungary. Along with his brother Xavier, he served in the Belgian Army during the First World War. He carried out secret negotiations on behalf of the Emperor in 1917, in an unsuccessful attempt to obtain a separate peace for Austria-Hungary without the knowledge of Germany.

Charles I of Austria by Bain News Service - the United States Library of Congress's Prints and Photographs division

Emperor Charles (Karl) I of Austria (King Charles IV of Hungary) (1887-1922) was the last ruler of the Austro-Hungarian Empire, becoming the heir of his grand-uncle Franz-Joseph after the assassination of his uncle, Archduke Franz Ferdinand in 1914. He presided over the dissolution of the Empire after the end of the First World War in 1918, when his plan to restructure Austria-Hungary as a federation consisting of autonomous ethnic states was rejected by the victorious Allies. In 1922, while living in exile on the island of Madeira, he developed pneumonia and died at the age of 34.

Franz von Papen –
the German Federal Archive (Deutsches Bundesarchiv)

Franz von Papen (1879-1969) A Catholic Center Party politician, he served as Chancellor of Germany for a brief period in 1932. Papen was largely responsible for persuading the aging President of the Weimar Republic, Paul von Hindenburg, to name Adolf Hitler as Chancellor in 1933. Papen served as Vice-Chancellor in the Hitler government from 1933-34. He escaped assassination on the infamous Night of the Long Knives (June 30, 1934) through the intervention of Hermann Goering, then later was appointed as Ambassador to Austria and Turkey by the Nazi government.

Mihaly Karolyi by Cecile Tormay

Mihaly Karolyi (1875-1955) son of wealthy Hungarian aristocrats who became a left-wing politician and leader of the Party of Independence and 1848. He was the last Prime Minister of the Kingdom of Hungary, which came to an end in November 1918, and subsequently was the Provisional President of the short-lived Hungarian Democrat Republic until March, 1919. He went into exile from Hungary in 1919, and did not return until 1946. He served as Ambassador to France from 1947-1949.

Istvan Tisza by Gyula Benczúr

Istvan Tisza (1861-1918) was a conservative politician, a member of the Liberal Party, who served two terms as Prime Minister of Hungary (1903-1905, and 1913-1917) under Emperors Franz Joseph and Charles. He opposed Austria-Hungary's entry to the war in 1914, but thereafter supported the war to the end. He was shot to death in his home by political opponents in 1918.

Adolf Hitler as a young man - University of North Carolina

Adolf Hitler (1889-1945) was a native of Austria who served in the German Army in the First World War. He was a twice-decorated war hero, winning the Iron Cross First and Second Class. He began his political career when, after the war he was employed by the Army to infiltrate the German Workers Party (later renamed National Socialist German Workers Party, or Nazi Party), of which he later became the leader. Hitler gave himself the nickname "Wolf", and it was subsequently incorporated in the names of several of his military headquarters, the most famous being Wolf's Lair (*"Wolfsshannze"*) in East Prussia, the scene of a famous assassination attempt in 1944.

Admiral Horthy - Wikipedia.

Mikilos Horthy (1868-1957) rose to the rank of Admiral and command of the Austro-Hungarian Navy by 1918, after starting the war as a Captain. He gained control of the National Army after briefly serving as Minister of War under the counter-revolutionary government of Gyula Károlyi in 1919. In 1920 the National Assembly replaced the Democratic Republic of Hungary with a renewed Kingdom of Hungary, but it was made clear by the Entente Powers that Hungary would not be permitted to restore Charles IV to the throne. The Assembly, surrounded by units of the National Army under Horthy's command therefore offered the former Admiral the title of Regent, with vast, almost dictatorial powers. He led Hungary into an alliance with Germany in World War II, and was deposed and arrested after the war.

Édouard Herriot 01 - the United States Library of Congress's Prints and Photographs

Edouard Herriot (1872-1957) a member of the Radical Party, he served three times as Prime Minister of the Third Republic between the World Wars. He also held many other ministerial posts and was the President of the National assembly after the Second World War from 1947 to 1954.

Wilhelm Groener by Pahl, Georg –
the German Federal Archive (Deutsches Bundesarchiv)

Wilhelm Groener (1867-1939) became the *de facto* commander of the German Army in 1918 after the overthrow of the war dictatorship of Eric Ludendorff, and before the Armistice. He used the Army to crush a Communist revolution in Germany in 1918-1919, then later, as Minister of War under the Social Democrat Ebert, attempted without success to subordinate the Army to the civil government of the Weimar Republic. He served as Transportation Minister, Defense Minister and Interior Minister with various governments between 1919 and 1939.

Kaiser Wilhelm II: see *High Tide in Martinique*
Raymond Gram Swing: see *High Tide in Martinique*
Rupprecht Maria Luitpold Ferdinand, Crown Prince of Bavaria: see *High Tide in Martinique*
Winston Churchill: see *High Tide in Martinique*
Frank Lowden: see *High Tide in Martinique*
Joseph McCormick: see *High Tide in Martinique*
Leonard Wood: see *High Tide in Martiniqu*

e

ABOUT THE AUTHOR

Andrew Heller is a retired trial attorney, is married and is the father of two children and a chinchilla. He has a Master's Degree in European History (Purdue University, 1982), and has been studying the World Wars and the inter-war period for a half-century.

43693140R00148

Made in the USA
Lexington, KY
09 August 2015